A Whisper of Leaves

Ashley Capes

For Brooke

Chapter 1

Riko unclenched her fist when the plastic of her phone cover creaked.

"Damn it."

She dropped it on the empty passenger seat and took a breath. Relax, idiot. Smart phones aren't cheap. She gripped the steering wheel of her little Toyota instead; was he ever coming out?

Parked beneath the shade of a pine tree in one of Fuji-Yoshida's better neighbourhoods, it probably looked like she was on a stake out – the family who'd circled the block in the afternoon sun had certainly given her an odd look.

But she didn't have a choice; her job was at stake, maybe more.

And the man who held everything in his palm was doing his best to stay out of sight. Ikeda's compound – the residence was more than merely 'fenced' – had cameras, intercoms and a massive gate that remained closed to visitors. He had to leave sometime. Or return, if he was out. And she'd waited hours – she wasn't going anywhere, especially after nearly getting lost finding the place.

What would she even say? He'd be angry. And he wouldn't believe her; why would he? Her word against that of his son. She was a fool for trying.

Riko jumped when her phone rang. She grabbed it.

Dad.

"No way." Not now. She jammed the mute button down and tossed the phone back onto the seat. Even if she could talk, he wasn't going to say anything she hadn't heard a thousand times before. Worse than a broken record – he was like some awful, auditory tattoo.

A black Lexus, sleek as a gymnast, pulled into the driveway. Riko jumped out of the Toyota and dashed across the road, slipping between Lexus and gate. The driver, a man in a dark hat and suit, hit the horn and inched the car forward.

Riko stood her ground. "I need to speak to Ikeda-sama."

The driver pulled on the handbrake before winding the window down. "What are you doing?" he called.

"I need to speak to Ikeda-sama. It's important."

He stepped out of the car, leaving it running. "He doesn't take visitors. Best if you get out of the way, young lady."

"Please."

He shook his head, then looked over his shoulder. "Shachō?"

A back door opened and a short man exited. Of an age with her father, his hair matched the jet black frames of his glasses. A blue tie sat bright against the grey of his suit. "Konda? What is this?"

"This lady here wants to talk to you. She won't move, I'm

sorry."

Riko gave a bow. "Ikeda-sama. I wanted to speak to you about your son."

The man's expression morphed from annoyance to suspicion. His narrowed eyes tracked her as she stepped closer. Konda too, kept a close watch.

"How does this regard Yuuki?" Ikeda's posture would have brought a coat rack to tears.

"I taught at –"

"Enough." He held up a hand. "You are Riko-san?"

"Yes. And I came to swear to you that I never acted in an inappropriate manner with Yuuki."

Konda whistled, but looked down when Ikeda glared at him. To Riko, Ikeda said, "This is a poor apology."

"It must be hard to believe, but I'm telling the truth. Maybe the pressure on him was –"

He shook his head. "You do not hail from Japan originally, do you? I hear a slight accent. English? No, Australian perhaps?"

She frowned. "My parents are from Hokaido, but they moved to Melbourne before I was born."

He nodded, showing no pleasure at his guesswork, skilful as it was. "Then you are here on a work permit."

"Yes, but that doesn't have anything to do with what happened."

He smiled. "Do you think so? My son is not a liar. Should you wish to remain here in Fuji-Yoshida, in Japan for that matter, you will keep away from my family and my home."

Remain in Japan? Could he actually get her deported? "But –"

"Understand, Riko-san, that I will not have this disgrace

fall upon the Ikeda name. Consider yourself fortunate that you were only dismissed."

"That's not –"

Ikeda pointed at her. "Not another word." He climbed back into the Lexus and snapped an order. The gates rattled open and Konda returned to the driver's seat, giving her a look. A warning? Part sympathy – it was so fleeting she couldn't be sure.

Riko stepped aside and the car lurched forward.

And that was that.

Chapter 2

Riko paused on the forest trail, the ache in her calves and the sweat trickling down her back signs enough. She dumped her pack on dark leaves and unzipped her jumper, which helped a little. She turned a slow circle, breathing deep. A whole year teaching English in Fuji-Yoshida and she was only now setting foot inside the national park, only now coming close to Mt Fuji. Not that the mountain was visible through the tangle of trees yet. Green limbs, green leaves, green everywhere, and the earthy rot of leaves underfoot. But nice. On a fallen log the moss was soft beneath her fingertips and gentle light fought through the canopy, even the stick she carried was perfect for hiking.

"I'm glad you thought of this, Kiyomi."

Her friend grinned, shrugging her way out of a powder-blue coat. Her short hair was damp with sweat at her temples and neck. "Me too. It's just so hot, even in here."

"You're doing better than me." Riko smiled back. "It's good to get my mind off work too." Her smile faded. "And if I still had a job, that'd mean something."

"I still think the school is wrong to punish you. You didn't do anything."

"It's his word against mine."

"It's still not fair."

Riko shrugged. "How far to Saiko?"

"Not far." She grinned. "Just how unfit are you?"

"Yeah?" Riko bent and scooped a clump of dirt, throwing it at Kiyomi, who ducked as she laughed.

They'd already been hiking for hours and her legs and back were weary – a good weariness, but a little rest wouldn't hurt. She took a drink from her backpack and tipped it back, cool water soothing her throat. Sweat slicked the back of her neck; she'd tied her hair up into a pony tail but it didn't make much difference, even in the cool beneath the trees.

"How come Daisuke couldn't come?"

"He's with his parents but he promised to visit tonight," Kiyomi said, putting her own water away. "Ready?"

"Yep."

Kiyomi set off again, the scrape of her feet loud. There was so little sound in the forest – no animals, no wind. The trees were just so dense; almost oppressive – as if the rest of the world had slipped away beyond the green.

"Know any short cuts?" Riko asked.

Kiyomi laughed. "No, not really."

"Then let's find one, I'm getting hungry. What direction's the lake? You said it was close." Riko hopped off the trail, climbing an uneven mound of broken ground where an old tree had woven its roots around cracks of volcanic rock.

"Riko, no!"

She spun. "What?"

"Come back." Kiyomi gestured, almost frantic.

Riko climbed down. "Kiyomi?"

"You shouldn't leave the path."

"Why not? Geez, are we in a horror movie?"

"No, seriously. You might find something you won't like."

"Oh. You mean, because of the suicides?" Riko glanced at the pale trunks; how many bodies would the rangers find this year? Last year it'd been over sixty. "No-one really talks about it much."

She nodded, lowering her voice. "Sometimes hikers find things like photos or notes or empty pill casings. Daisuke found a body once."

"That's crazy." Riko shivered. Sunlight still slipped through the leaves but the shadows seemed thicker now. Deeper. And over there, between a mossy stump and another fissure in the ground...was that something moving? Stupid. Probably just an animal – except she hadn't seen any all morning. Not even a bird.

"Well, I doubt we'll see anything." Kiyomi said. "It's supposed to be deeper in that you see those things. And not close to the lake like we are." She laughed, though to Riko it sounded a little forced. "Daisuke thinks Aokigahara's haunted and that older spirits are supposed to be here too. Unhappy ones."

"But you don't?"

She shrugged. "I guess not. But it's easy to get lost if you leave the trail and I don't want to see a dead body."

"Let's keep to the path then."

The trail crested a long hill. Damp leaves coated the sharp slope on the other side, and she slid halfway down, hands grasping for purchase as her rear bumped and scraped the earth. Kiyomi slid too, but handled it better. Riko's sweat chilled at the bottom of the slope, the sun failing to penetrate leaves in the hollow. Kiyomi picked up the pace and within moments, the trees thinned. A marker appeared, standing in weathered blue. Close to the lake now. Light reflected in the distance, flashing between twisted trunks.

"I can see the water."

"Good, I'm a little hungry myself." Kiyomi's relief had a strained edge. Riko couldn't blame her friend; her own voice was probably the same. Something about the forest, when the sun snuck behind a cloud...

The walking trail exited the trees above a large open area dotted with tables and benches. The grass was cut close; the water's edge a brilliant deep blue. Across the lake, clear of snow, loomed Mt Fuji – a dark purple giant. Almost glorious, the way it hogged the skyline, seemingly unconcerned with everything below it. Even its reflection in the silken surface of the lake was proud.

"Beautiful, isn't it?"

Riko nodded. There was a new stillness, just looking at it – how close, yet how distant its peak. She should climb it one day, even if she wasn't that fit.

"Let's eat." Kiyomi strode to one of the tables and unpacked lunch. "I'm surprised no-one is here." Riko sat across the table and accepted an obento package, digging in to the rice ball. The sun warmed her back and she stared at Fuji's reflection as she chewed.

"So what are you going to do now?" Kiyomi asked around a mouthful.

"Stay away from Ikeda-san, for a start." Riko said.

"What?" Kiyomi paused, food halfway to her mouth. "You never mentioned that."

"I went to his house yesterday. I had to try something."

"What happened?"

"He was ready to pounce on my visa. Said his son wasn't a liar and told me never to come back, or he'd make sure I'd be going home. He sounded like he meant it."

"He did. Don't go there again. He's a powerful man, Riko."

"Yes, Mum."

Kiyomi frowned. "I mean it, Riko. I'm worried. He knows *everyone.*"

"Don't be worried. I've got three months to find something. I can always offer private lessons for a while." Her contract with Yamanashi Language Centre forbade taking private students, but that didn't matter now. Still, she couldn't stop a sigh. Private tutoring wouldn't amount to much. Her position at the Centre hadn't been too bad – she taught mostly professional adults and senior high schoolers looking for extension work, people who actually wanted to learn. Mostly anyway. Some of the men were a little... forward and she'd had to put a stop to that. But the work had been enough to support herself.

And now, with spring break soon to be over, she'd be going back to nothing, instead of a secure job.

"Can you try another branch? Travel to work?"

She shook her head. "Fujita-san isn't just director of the local centre, he runs the whole network."

"Typical. I could try get you a few shifts at Uni. The library's giving the PhD students as much work as they can take lately."

"That might help, thanks." She lowered a kiwi-half and spoon. "I might have to ring Mum and borrow some money."

Kiyomi raised an eyebrow. "Do you really want to do

that?"

"No. And if Dad found out, he'd jump on a plane and drag me back to Australia. It'd be all the proof he needed that I can't take care of myself."

She placed a hand over Riko's. "I wouldn't let that happen."

Riko made to thank her but stopped. The scent of wood smoke drifted through the trees. "Can you smell that?"

"What?"

She stood. "Smoke."

Kiyomi followed. "Over there." She pointed to the tree line, to the right of where they'd entered the clearing. A faint smudge hung in the treetops until the soft breeze did away with it. Riko headed for the forest.

"Wait."

"It could be a fire." Ducking into the shade, Riko followed a narrow path until she lost the scent of smoke. She backtracked and found Kiyomi looking around the trail. Riko pointed. "There. It's deeper. Off the path."

Kiyomi crossed her arms. "Bad idea."

"Shouldn't we put it out if it's a campfire?"

"Maybe, but we could get lost."

"We just have to mark out a trail, right? Like you told me?"

Kiyomi threw up her hands. "All right, very clever. Wait a minute." She dug into her bag and drew out a pocket knife. She cut an 'x' into the bark. "I shouldn't be doing this. It's a National Park."

"No-one will know." Riko climbed over a moss-covered log, tracking the scent of smoke. She detoured deep fissures in the ground, pausing only for Kiyomi to slash another marker or two.

Through the trees she saw no smoke, but the scent remained.

Kiyomi slowed. "We should have found the fire by now."

Riko paused. Kiyomi was right. Smoke wouldn't have reached the clearing at all, if it wasn't thicker here, deeper into the trees. "Maybe we should turn back?"

Kiyomi smiled. "I thought you wanted to put out the fire?"

"I can still smell it. It's stronger." She tossed her stick into the undergrowth. "But there's nothing here."

"There." Kiyomi clambered across a mess of tree roots. Riko leant over. Beyond a broad tree trunk a small orange blaze burned clean. It was a pile of leaves, resting beneath an oak. What little smoke rose from the pile was caught by the canopy, branches spreading wide.

Riko crept forward, Kiyomi at her side.

The ground around the fire had been raked. Not a single stray leaf rested on the forest floor. Closest to the trunk lay thick loam, it too, neat.

"There's no-one here," Riko whispered. "Should we go closer?"

"This is weird."

Footsteps swished through grass. A tall man strode into view, steel rake in hand. His clothes were faded but hardly shabby, and his white hair grew in a firm wave. He stood over the blaze. Were his eyes moist?

"What's he doing?" Kiyomi said as she crouched. "Is he some sort of ranger?" Her eyes were wide.

"I don't know. Maybe we should go."

Riko turned, choosing each step carefully and trying to use the broad tree as a screen. She cast frequent glances over her shoulder. Kiyomi duplicated her steps and Riko held her breath until they put some distance between them and the odd man. Then she quickened her stride, moving from mark to mark until she tripped.

Riko broke her fall with both hands, scraping the loam as she hit. A spider slipped from a curled leaf and she flinched back with a cry.

Kiyomi put a hand on her shoulder. "Are you all right? What is it?"

"I'm okay, yeah. Just a spider." She sat up, wiping her hands with a shiver. "I hope he didn't hear anything."

"He seemed lost in his own world."

Riko pushed to her knees and stopped. Something rectangular poked from where she'd torn into the ground. She brushed leaves and dirt aside, giving the spider a frown as it scurried away.

A book. Bound in leather, its pages yellowed, stained and mostly stuck together. How long had it been buried on the forest floor?

"Look at this." She held it up.

Kiyomi took it, turning it over in her hands. "Wow. I'm surprised it's still in one piece. It looks old. Even without the grime."

Riko accepted the book when Kiyomi held it out. "Should I leave it?"

"I would."

"Do you think it's...you know?"

She frowned. "No way to know. You should leave it."

But she didn't want to just put it back beneath the earth to rot away. It looked like a journal. A fascinating story could lurk inside. And what were the chances of her tripping at exactly the right point to uncover it? No. It had to come home.

"I think I'll take it."

"If you say so."

"No-one's going to miss it, are they?"

Kiyomi shrugged, then held out her hand. She pulled Riko up. "Let's just get out of here, all right? That old guy was strange, burning leaves out in the middle of no-where."

Riko nodded. "You're right about that."

Chapter 3

Kiyomi wouldn't touch the journal when they returned. Even Daisuke was unwilling to read it when he arrived. It was obvious Kiyomi thought Riko was being disrespectful to the dead for keeping it. And maybe she was.

But Riko couldn't stop reading.

The pages were mostly stuck together, but with her hairdryer and nail file she managed to read some of the journal. Many entries were simple observations of events and times. Others were messages directed to an unnamed 'you' and yet other entries, the kanji often smeared, were haiku and sometimes senryu.

It took her over an hour, but she finally translated one into English, just for fun:

> *black clouds*
> *brooding*
> *was I ever a bird?*

Not a cheerful piece. Riko set the pen down. How long had she sat there, hunched over the journal? Jimmy Stewart looked down on her from a *Rear Window* poster resting between bookshelves that formed an arch over her desk. It was usually a cosy arch, but it had become oppressive. She leant back, putting her feet up on the desk. Her socks were a splash of blue against the shelves. One question remained unanswered; why had the writer gone to Aokigahara? What went wrong with her life? In one of the passages, the diary-owner described scenting her hair with jasmine and surprising her husband. She sounded happy then, at least.

Someone tapped on her screen door.

Riko's desk chair squeaked as she put her feet down and spun. "Come in."

Kiyomi slid the screen open. She wore a floral dressing gown and even from across the room the scent of orange shampoo was strong. Daisuke stood behind her, his ready smile absent. His hair was suddenly bleach-blonde.

"Hey, when did you do that?"

He ran a hand through his hair. "Ah, a bit earlier – what do you think?"

"It looks good, kinda 1990s."

He gave half a smile but it didn't last when he caught sight of the journal. Kiyomi's expression was one of concern. "Riko, we've been calling your name."

"Sorry. I'm lost in the journal. What's up?"

Daisuke glanced at Kiyomi, who shrugged. He sighed. "This might sound a bit strange, but have you been humming?"

"No, why?"

"Well, Kiyomi and I heard humming from this end of the apartment."

"I haven't heard it. Are you sure?"

"We're sure." Kiyomi said.

"And you both heard it?"

Daisuke nodded. "It sounded like a woman humming, but it wasn't your voice."

"And the tune was old, like something from an old war movie," Kiyomi added. "I don't know if you'd have grown up with the song in Australia."

"Maybe it was a neighbour's TV?"

"Could be." Kiyomi nodded slowly then took Daisuke's arm. "I guess that could be it. Well, we're heading out soon. Are you sure you don't want to come?"

"I'm fine, thanks."

"All right, see you later."

Riko returned to the book. Barely half a dozen words into the next entry and she stood. Her neck was tight and eyes dry; it took more than a few blinks to clear her vision. Time for a proper break. She still hadn't showered since the hike. Grabbing a towel and ducking into hall, she moved to the bathroom and paused in the enclosure to strip down. She filled the tub in the 'wet' room then grabbed the shower nozzle and sat on the wooden bench where she soaped up and blasted hot water. Everything took a lot longer than showering back home but it was worth it. Once she was clean, she hopped into the bath for a soak, giving a long sigh as she settled in. The heat soothed her calves and aching feet.

Money was going to be a problem soon.

Odd how such thoughts always came from out of nowhere. As if her subconscious had been wrestling them quietly, pouncing the moment she relaxed.

Diving into the journal had to be an avoidance technique. She hadn't studied pysch but it sounded about right. Calling home for help wasn't an option. Even family in Japan was out. Aunt Eiko would eventually tell Mum.

If she could find work quick enough, it'd be fine. Hopefully some of her old students would want a tutor. She hadn't even had a chance to say goodbye. What was her sponsor telling people? And would Ikeda leave her alone? Was her visit a mistake?

Once dressed, Riko had the house to herself. In the small kitchen she put some water on the stove and collected herbs, placing the bundle on a chopping board beside a small knife. Before she made a single chop, her phone interrupted.

Mum.

Riko took a deep breath, dragging strength in with it.

"Hi, Mum."

"Riko-chan. Why haven't you returned my calls? Or your father's?"

"I've been busy, Mum. I'm sorry." No point mentioning the bad news.

"Eiko said you moved out. More than three months ago."

Riko rolled her eyes, dumping the knife into the sink. Aunt Eiko had done pretty good to hold out so long – Riko had moved out much earlier. "Of course I did. I'm a grown woman."

"A grown woman would be married by now."

"Mum, this isn't about Ryuu is it?"

"It's about all of your relationships, dear. And he was a fine young man."

"Mum."

"You're wasting time and with your father getting worse." She sighed from the other end of the phone. "I want him to see you happy."

"That's not what he wants."

A gasp. "Of course it is. Now, you listen to me. Your father's stubborn, but the doctors thought he should go back to hospital. Who knows what will happen?" Her mother's voice held a note of deep concern that she would never admit aloud. It had been the same, even before Riko left home. But there were good hospitals in Melbourne; everyone knew that. And if Dad was back in hospital, that was probably the best place for him. Same as last time. Mum was just laying on the guilt again. How far away was the demand for Riko to come home? To be more dutiful?

The water started boiling over. "I have to go, Mum. I'm cooking."

"It could be serious this time, you know that."

"Mum, I'll call you tomorrow." Riko didn't wait for a response. She hung up, leaving her phone on the kitchen table. The water hissed where it hit the hotplate, and she lifted it off the heat and wiped the bottom.

Was Dad really sick? He'd tried to call, after all. Maybe hanging up was a bit much.

But he was always in and out of hospital. He always got better and he always got sick again too. And so his lectures were always 'from his death bed' as he'd claim. Not this time. She didn't need to hear it again.

A thump from the other room.

Riko froze. It wasn't the neighbours this time. No humming from a TV or radio. It came from her bedroom. Kiyomi and Daisuke were still out, and would be hours yet. Her fingers slipped around the handle of the heaviest knife in the block and she moved into the hall. With each soft step, her heart jumped a beat.

The door was still open, but the light off. Had she turned it off?

Riko clenched the knife. Her arm shook as she reached out to flick the switch.

Empty.

Not a single rumple on her bed. The journal and her papers were in place. The tiny wardrobe was empty. Riko stalked into the hall and hit another light switch, checking Kiyomi's room with its ordered lines and single, innocuous Hello Kitty ornament, then the rest of the house. Even the toilet. Nothing. No-one.

She put the knife back and returned to her desk. Nothing was out of place so what made the sound? She was alone, that much she'd proved. She shook her head; should finish cooking. Or maybe translate some more of the journal. Or better yet, forget the food and journal and get some sleep. Riko rolled her pen across the desktop. The clatter of it filled the room.

She stopped.

Something *was* out of place.

Her mother's picture lay flat on the dresser.

Chapter 4

She waited all night but there were no more strange sounds.

Wrapped in a blanket on the couch with a knife close by, bad movies and apples and coffee kept her awake. She'd even checked between couch cushions for spiders.

Kiyomi never returned; she had obviously stayed at Daisuke's. Now that daylight finally blasted through the windows, Riko stumbled into the kitchen found a packet of dried fruit in the pantry and threw it onto the bench. She rubbed her eyes. "Stupid."

She'd let the dark, and being alone, spook her.

She poured another coffee to go with her dry breakfast and perched at the table, one knee held to her chest. If only she had another hike to go on. Anything to stop her driving by Yamanashi Language Centre. Maybe if she hid her car keys, stayed indoors? Went all *hikikomori* – became a real shut in? No. Something else. Reading the journal wasn't much of an idea either; her eyes were wobbling in their sockets, the whites probably more 'smashed strawberry.'

Not the best day for job hunting either.

But maybe the kind of day for visiting. Maybe Yuuki Ikeda would be at the park today. How such a part time job didn't shame the precious Ikeda-san, she didn't know. The life of a third son – no-one really cared what he did, she supposed, so long as it was unremarkable. In fact, it further supported his father's reaction. It was all about what her supposed transgression would do to *him*, not his son.

But if she could get Yuuki alone, maybe she could talk some sense into him. Tell him to speak to his father. Maybe get her job back.

It was worth a shot.

And yet, if Ikeda found out…

She paused, coffee cup half-lowered, skin prickling. "Bad idea, Riko."

But what else could she do? Nothing. And no-one could help her. No way she'd end up a burden to Kiyomi, she had to try. Riko showered, not taking time to soak in the tub, and dressed in a flash. She leapt into her shoes in the entryway and snatched up her keys and bag before jumping into the car. All she had to do was find Yuuki and explain what he'd done with his lie. Appeal to his sense of fairness. If he had any. Damn kid. Riko gripped the wheel and the leather creaked.

Fuji-Yoshida Park was busy. Cherry blossoms and people drifted over the soft grass and beneath the slap-to-the-face-sun; any shade was welcome. One young couple laid together, their books forgotten. A businessman shovelled down a bowl of noodles, beside him a woman nursed a coffee, tapping her feet to whatever song she'd plugged into via her iPod.

A gardener crested a small rise at the centre of the park,

his green uniform and hat conspicuous – surrounded as he was by colourful tops and bare-skinned legs. Still in jeans, Riko huffed. Sweat was already forming at her temples.

"Hi, could you help me find someone? He works for the Park."

The man squinted at her. "Yes?"

"Yuuki Ikeda?"

"Oh, him." He gestured with his hand, toward a modest building nestled beneath the spreading branches of the cherry trees. The steel roof was littered with white and pink spots. "He'll be sharpening tools in there."

Riko thanked him and strode across the lawn. She paused at the door; grinding sounds came from inside. She timed her knocks between the tool's bursts. Hurry up.

"Coming."

Her jaw ached as she waited. Yuuki finally opened the door, a welder's mask in hand. He paled and then glanced away, suddenly looking half his age, not just about to hit college – but like a primary school kid who'd been caught in a lie. Which he had.

"Riko-chan." Yuuki gaped. "Riko-san, I mean Riko-san."

"Stop that," she snapped. "This is serious, Yuuki. We need to talk about what you said."

"You're angry with me."

"Of course I'm –" She lowered her voice. "Of course I'm angry with you." Shock had definitely worn off. Anger sat in its place, straining on its leash.

"I – I'm sorry I tried to kiss you. And...tried to touch your breast." He finished in a rush and stared at his feet, cheeks aflame.

She folded her arms as if to brush away the memory

of his hesitant touch. "Forget about that. Why did you lie, Yuuki? You know I lost my job. I might even have to leave Japan if your father decides to force me out."

"I know, Riko-san."

"And?" Her hand twitched. How much worse would things get if she knocked him down? Or throttled him?

He glanced at her. His eyes were wide and his frown deep. "I don't even know why I did it."

"Well, what are you going to do about it?"

"Do you mean tell the truth?"

"What do you think?"

He trembled. "But my father will be furious; he'll tear me to pieces."

"Shit, Yuuki..." She stopped with a sigh. Of course he was afraid of his father. Poor kid. God damn it, he'd screwed up but maybe she could ease up a bit. After all, she knew what that was like. The disappointment of a father..."Yuuki, I need your help. If you speak with Fujita-san maybe you can persuade him to keep the truth a secret from your father. He still might give me my job back. Or at least a decent referral letter."

He still couldn't meet her eyes. "Fujita-san and Dad are friends."

Riko threw her hands up. "Isn't that perfect then?" She strode off, ignoring his call.

*

Riko raised an eyebrow.

The journal was changing. The characters were drawn with less care, their subjects jumping wildly. There were more haiku and more single lines of confessions and accusations:

> *And with barely a twinge, it's done. I've betrayed your memory with another.*

Then on the very next page:

> *Your heart is never clear, is it? There's always a little cloud around it.*

And several pages later:

> *Today you brought me a flower. You'd grown it just for me, having hidden the pot in the garden for weeks. How I never noticed it!*

Still no name. But there was little doubt the narrator was a woman. Her unhappiness blinked through the pages, some sickly smooth beneath Riko's fingertips. Too many pages were stuck together or unreadable. She'd have to do more than air the pages by the window in order to open some of them, and her routine over the last couple of nights included sweeping grains of dirt and membrane-like fragments of leaves into her waste-paper basket before bed.

Days had slipped into one another. She slept and read and translated, ate and slept. Sometimes she met Kiyomi for coffee, sometimes she shopped for the apartment and despite searching each day for another job, she found nothing. Not even tutoring. Not a single one of her ex-students responded to her offer. Was it the contract the Centre had everyone – teachers and students – sign before commencing lessons? Or Ikeda's influence?

Riko stood, stretching her back. She moved closer to the bed and bent to touch her toes, holding the position a moment.

She straightened.

Smoke.

Riko dashed into the hallway. No sign of fire or smoke. Yet an acrid scent stung her eyes and rasped down her throat. She stopped in the kitchen, coughing. The oven and stove were cold and the TV silent. She fell to her knees, gagging. Invisible smoke? Was it even real? And where the hell was it coming from?

She pulled her shirt up over her mouth and crawled into the lounge, blinking through tears. It was so thick! Riko hacked as she scrambled forward, knocking into a shelf. Something sharp bit into her scalp and she swore. Another picture frame.

Riko picked it up and the smoke was gone.

A rush of clean air hit her lungs. She wiped at the blur of tears and slumped back, legs crossed, jaw slack.

A little blood marred the edge of the frame, and her head throbbed, but the image in the frame...Kiyomi's father. He stood at Lake Saiko, an arm around his daughter. He smiled, but the flash caught on the lens of his glasses, concealing his eyes.

Riko breathed hard.

Was it a sign?

No. She was crazy. Crazy as a street preacher. Only her eyes weren't bulging and her outfit wasn't Charlie Chaplin-esque Tramp. Had the photo stopped the invisible smoke? It didn't make sense. Hallucinations? A mental breakdown maybe – but from what? Losing a job wasn't enough. Shit, had someone poisoned her? Some freak slipping something into the city's water-system?

She knew the likelihood of that.

Riko climbed to her feet, replaced the photo and headed to the bathroom enclosure where she jammed the plug in the basin and ran cold water to the top. Then she dunked her head, wincing as a chill soaked into the cut – and exhaled. Bubbles spun and threshed around her face, tickling her skin.

All right, Riko. Keep calm.

She raised her head, sucking in air. Beautiful, clean air. Water ran down her neck and dripped from her nose, soaking the front of her old Astro Boy shirt. A shiver rippled up from her toes, along her legs and into her spine. What was going on? First the humming, then the picture on the dresser and now imaginary smoke and yet another photo frame falling from furniture?

Kiyomi could confirm it when she came home for lunch. Riko could get her to check for remnants of smoke. And if Kiyomi could smell it – then no-one had to be hallucinating.

Riko pulled the plug and went back to her room, slumping into her desk chair. She rested her head in her hands, fingers avoiding the throbbing cut. Her hair fell across the journal and she flinched back.

A pair of kanji on the page seemed to shimmer.

Yurei.

Dim. Soul.

Chapter 5

Kiyomi paced the lounge with a slight furrow to her brow. Light from round paper lamps on the roof cast shadows across her face. Finally, she slumped onto one of the tatami mats with a sigh, arm resting on the coffee table.

Riko leant forward from her perch on the edge of the couch. "Well?"

"No, I still don't smell any smoke. Are you sure?"

"I'm sure."

"And my father's picture hit you on the head?"

"It did. Hurt too." Riko forced a smile.

Kiyomi gave her a look. "Riko, you know I'm your friend, don't you?"

"I do know that." Not a promising start to a conversation.

"I think you might be having a bit of a breakdown. You know, after being fired."

Riko turned to the darkened TV. Why not? It made more sense than imaginary smoke. "Maybe."

"I know you think everything's connected – the lake, the smoke and the man with the leaves, the photos of our parents, the humming and whatever – but I'm not convinced."

"What do you think's happening?" Riko asked.

"Nothing. I think you've stressed yourself into this... episode."

Wonderful. Crazy at twenty-seven. "So I should see a doctor?"

She took a deep breath, obviously uncomfortable at the mention of doctors. "Probably. At least, if it happens again." Riko's shoulders slumped.

Kiyomi came over and hugged her, squeezing her around the middle. "I'll take the afternoon off. We'll go to lunch."

"You don't have to do that."

She smiled. "I want to."

Lunch was sushi in a busy cafe with a clear view of Fuji, a blue shadow in the distance. Riko chewed slowly as Kiyomi chattered. AC/DC was playing over the speakers and at a nearby table an older couple sat together, each with a paper, working on Nonograms – the man's grid was nearly complete; a boy kicking a soccer ball.

Wait, was that a question in the stream of words? She looked back to Kiyomi. "Huh?"

Kiyomi slid her food aside. "It doesn't matter. So, you're still thinking about it?"

"Trying not to, actually."

"You need to get your mind off it."

"It felt real. My eyes watered."

Kiyomi sighed. "How's your father?"

"Gee, thanks. That's much better."

Her friend waited.

"Apparently he's in the hospital again."

Kiyomi straightened. "Wait, you didn't say anything. Is he all right? What's wrong?"

"Mum didn't say, but he'll be fine." He always was. Once, during her last year of high school, he was admitted and released from hospital twice in one afternoon. For 'stress-related' ailments. No-one had any idea what was wrong; not doctors, nor her mother, and least of all him. And yet, he never complained.

Not about his health anyway.

"Should you visit?"

"No, it's not that bad. Mum would say." Riko clenched her toes inside her sandals; she would have rung back if there was a real problem.

"So what about work then? What are you going to do?"

Riko drew warm cafe air in through her nose. That was a problem. "I don't know. I won't bother to ask for a referral, but I'll look again tomorrow. I could try retail."

"Not many shops hiring at the moment."

"No?"

"That's what I hear on campus. Barely any casual work going."

"Good. Another challenge."

"There's still the library with me."

"I dunno if I can take your hours."

"Think about it. I can afford a pay cut, you know."

Riko took a sip of her juice and nodded, glancing out the window.

*

Showa University would not make time for her. The best offer from one of its secretaries was a meeting with some dean, over a month away. Riko took the appointment anyway, keeping her shoulders rigid, killing a shrug before it happened. A month? Who knew where she'd be in a month.

The big companies were worse. They all wanted someone to train their staff in English, but none of her interviews yielded results – and she'd attended enough over the last few days.

Shinkin Bank was a real highlight.

Twenty minutes early and her sharpest shirt, the grey pencil skirt, black heels and her hair in a neat bun – and all for nothing. The interview itself went well. One woman sat forward, impressed at Riko's fluency in English. Even so, Riko had to mangle the truth, propping it up with some fast talking, as she glossed over her reasons for leaving Fuji-Yoshida's branch of the Yamanashi Language Centre.

She passed Ikeda-san on the way out.

He sent her a deep frown as he strode by. Riko groaned inside. Of course he knew someone at the bank. He knew everyone. And now he would sabotage her. From a sense of duty, no doubt. To Ikeda, she was not fit to teach. He doubtless thought he was doing the right thing.

He'd probably enjoy it though.

Riko crossed the congested footpath, paused for a motorbike then dashed across the street to her Toyota. Jumping in, she lay back a moment before thumping the steering wheel. "Damn it!" And damn Yuuki and his father. And Fujita-san, the coward.

She'd find something else. Or someone else. Aunt Eiko? No. She wouldn't be able to help, but even if she could, it was a bad idea. Eiko would tell Mum, and then that would be it. Dad would know and she'd be summoned home by a tractor beam of disappointment and concern. With a bit of smugness thrown in too.

Riko drove home, kicked her shoes off in the entryway and dumped her bag on the bed. At the desk she opened the journal. Better than job hunting. Kiyomi was out and the apartment quiet. The distant murmur from the highway snuck through the windows. The neighbours were silent.

Not a single trace of smoke.

The last few nights had been the same; no smoke, no humming, nothing falling. Kiyomi had even slept beside Riko's bed in her sleeping bag that first night. Riko failed to convince Kiyomi that she was fine, but talking late into the night like a couple of high school girls on a sleepover was exactly what she'd needed.

A large chunk of the journal's pages were stuck together. Even with her trusty nail file and hair dryer, she couldn't separate them. And it was during a critical part of the narrator's life. There might have been some clue as to who the woman was. Maybe someone at the library could help? So far she'd found three more haiku and one long entry. In Riko's own notebook, a slow picture was forming. A sombreness. Two people losing common ground.

> *old ice on the sill*
> *how once*
> *we could laugh*

Riko was collecting strands of straw, but barely a handful did not make a scarecrow. No-one was getting to Oz with that. But what she'd read was enough to hint at another important moment in the writer's life. One of the longer passages was equally revealing as the haiku.

> *Strange that I've become so much of someone else.*
> *During the war I knew who I was. In the perpetual*
> *red of smoke and flame, of running and hiding I*
> *knew. Once we got through, I knew. My future was*
> *a clear stream flowing from mountain to sea. Now*
> *I am so many puddles. You have a claim. He has a*
> *claim. And I am whatever is left, muddied with the*
> *love you both took.*

Riko rested her pen on the notepad, her finger hovering over a kanji in the journal. Options. Some symbols could be more than a few words. "Come on." She read the line, wrote a translation and changed her mind. Whether it was 'beak' or 'mouth' didn't matter too much:

> *blossom in your beak*
> *save some*
> *for the rest of us!*

A light moment, in a journal seemingly filled with so little respite. The next haiku, less so.

> *cold leaves —*
> *my cheek*
> *presses the dark*

Or was it too easy to read darkness into the verse, considering where the journal was found? Riko put a marker in and closed the book. Rolling her shoulders, she leant back, chair creaking.

Smoke.

Riko flung her chair back as she stood. It bounced off the end of the bed, and knocked her calf, but she was into the hall with a grunt. Thick grey tendrils staggered from Kiyomi's room, its screen ajar.

She hit the light as she entered, crouching beneath the smoke. It was the wardrobe; smoke poured from gaps in the door. Riko crawled along the carpet, squinting as she slid the door open and fell back.

A white and pink dress hung in a space of its own – Kiyomi's favourite. Somehow, smoke billowed from the fabric, as if pumped from a giant hose.

Smother it.

Riko snatched the dress and stepped toward the bed, only for the smoke to stop. The dress was bright, clean. It smelled brand new.

"God, what's happening?" she cried.

She threw the dress onto the bed and ran back to her room, where she snatched her bag and phone. At the door, she fumbled with shoes and keys and somehow managed to lock up before fleeing outside.

She jumped into her car and drove into the night.

Chapter 6

Riko lay on Aunt Eiko's couch, her pillow sinking. She rolled onto her back in the dark. A breath of light from the window caught on the steel of a light fitting. Her stomach was full and her hair washed. The couch was free of spiders, her night gown was fresh and the light blanket cool and clean against her skin.

The very house seemed to slow her pulse, ease her mind; she'd spent months here before finding a place with Kiyomi. Earlier she sent a text to her friend then explained to Eiko that she was giving her housemate some privacy for an anniversary. Eiko shook her head, muttering about 'young people'. Still, she'd smiled when Riko turned up on her doorstep, and bundled her up in a hug.

Tomorrow it was time to see someone. Anyone. Doctor, psychiatrist, counsellor, whatever. Just someone who could explain what was happening. Because it wasn't real. How could it be?

On the ceiling, the light grew. Passing cars? No – there were no engines. She propped herself onto her elbows. The light twisted into curling lines...and the lines became letters!

Riko blinked. Two bright words flickered across the ceiling.

Stop reading.

Stop reading what? The journal? She bit her tongue, squeezing her eyes shut. No way. It didn't matter. It was bullshit. There were no words up there. She was hallucinating. Stress-induced. Hypochondriac, just like Dad. She opened her eyes.

Nothing.

Slumping into the couch, Riko rolled to face the back cushions and fluffed her pillow. Just sleep. There's nothing there. She swallowed, staring into the dark.

Riko was roused from sleep as her aunt rummaged in the kitchen. She stretched, refusing to check the ceiling, and instead slid a screen open and met her aunt at the small kitchen table. The cool of the floor was soothing through her socks. Eiko brushed grey hair back from her face where she bent over the tea cups, one hand stirring. On the bench, her old silver kettle steamed – not unlike smoke. Riko clenched her jaw. None of that.

"Morning, dear."

"Good morning, Obasan." Riko put on a smile, though in truth, she didn't have to fake it. "Still stirring?"

"It's got to be perfect." Eiko set a cup of green tea before Riko and folded her hands before her own cup. "Your mother is worried about you."

"I'm doing okay. Just busy."

"You should call her. Your father isn't well."

Riko paused, cup at her lip. "Did she say something?"

"No, but I know Ryoko. She hates to worry people. It could be serious."

"I'll call her today."

"Good girl. Now, you better get ready for work. I won't have you being late on account of me." She waved her hands toward the bathroom. "I'll have something ready for you to eat when you're done."

"I've barely had two sips," Riko said.

"It'll be here, too. Go on."

Riko did as instructed, then finished her breakfast. Eiko had her out the door and on the way to 'work' in short order. Not one for small talk; it was just her way. And Riko wasn't going to stop to explain that she couldn't go to work. That little secret wasn't going anywhere.

She drove toward the downtown clinic. Sukiyaki was on the radio and she tapped along, mouthing the words as buildings rolled by. The light on the roof had told her to stop reading. Obviously the journal. A stern message from her subconscious maybe? That didn't make sense. She was unemployed but Kiyomi could support her, especially considering what her parents gave her. It wasn't right, but Kiyomi would insist.

It had to be something else. If not stress, then...

She'd found the journal in Aokigahara, a place where ghosts were said to linger. There was the strange humming, the invisible smoke and now words in light.

Was she being haunted?

"Ghosts, Riko?" And worse, she could now add 'talking to yourself' to the list of troubles.

It was an explanation. And maybe not a better one than going insane. Or maybe it was part of going insane? No matter that it was unlikely. Unlikely didn't explain everything that was happening. And if she did see a doctor, medication wouldn't fix it, would it? She slowed for an intersection, fighting a frown.

Something dark flashed in front of her windscreen.

Riko stomped on the brakes, tyres screeching. Had there been bright eyes in the shadow? Horns blared and she spun in the seat, heart pounding. Nothing. Only a growing row of cars lined up behind her – the man in the nearest was swearing and flinging his arms about.

She pulled into a supermarket and parked in the first empty space, breathing hard. The dark object seemed real. Nothing she could make out, but had there been a face? Shit. It couldn't have been real. It was stress. Her eyes playing tricks.

And yet, that didn't seem right. Something was going on. Something she wouldn't be able to explain to a doctor without being committed. Or medicated.

No. It had to be real. And there had to be another way to stop it.

Finally she laughed.

How stupid she'd been. Ghost stories 101. All she had to do was take the journal back to Aokigahara. So simple!

"There. Will that make you happy?" Riko demanded. Her shoulders turned to wonderful jelly. Much better. A way to put a stop to all the madness. She paused. Going back to Lake Saiko meant no more reading.

And maybe no more strange happenings.

Riko turned the key.

*

After explaining about Kiyomi's dress, Riko finished in a rush. "So I made an appointment today."

A lie. A small one, but enough to placate Kiyomi. And then maybe a psychiatrist after all. To be sure. But first, the forest. "I'm taking the journal back first though."

Kiyomi's arms were crossed. "Why? It doesn't make sense."

"I think it'll help."

"I doubt that."

She leant against the kitchen bench. "Please. Come with me, you know the trails."

Kiyomi uncrossed her arms and walked over. Her mouth was set. "I think you're wrong about this. Taking the journal back won't help, it's just feeding your..." She shook her head.

"My what?"

"Delusions. That's what they are. You're in trouble, Riko. This is serious." Her breath shuddered. "I'm really getting worried about you."

She took Kiyomi's hand and a laugh escaped. "Well I'm terrified."

"Then do what's right."

"I will. Once I take it back. It's the only way I can get it out of my head. I know myself, if I don't get rid of it I'll end up obsessed."

Kiyomi nodded. "Right, so let me throw it out. I'll even burn it if you want."

"It's my mess. Please, let me fix it."

Kiyomi pressed her lips together. "I can't miss more meetings with my supervisor."

"I can take a map."

"No." Kiyomi shook her head. "You'll probably get lost driving there, let alone inside the damn place. How about I ask Daisuke? We've hiked there a lot."

"Will he come?"

She fixed Riko with a stern look. "If he says 'yes,' I'm driving you to your appointment myself, all right?"

Riko nodded. "All right."

*

Heavy clouds crept across the sky and the sun was caught only in glimpses through the leaves. Riko trudged after Daisuke in the dim forest. The journal was a burden at the bottom of her backpack. The water, lunch and her coat, none of it weighed as much as the journal.

"It's much darker this time," she said.

Daisuke nodded, pausing to thump his hiking boots against a fallen log. Built up leaf clumps fell away. "If you go deeper it's black as night."

"You've left the paths before?"

"Just a few times."

Riko hesitated.

He shook his head, but he smiled too. "You want to know about the time I saw the body, right?"

"What was it like?" A gentle breeze dropped. The trees seemed to lean in, their twisted limbs twitching as leaves fell. Clouds smothered a patch of sunlight.

Daisuke shrugged. "Well, I only saw a skeleton. The plastic raincoat was still there, most of it was buried by leaves and moss. It was...bad. I felt bad for them. Wasn't there anyone who could help with whatever troubled them? I always wondered why they took a raincoat too. If they meant to come here to die, you know?"

"Yeah."

"I didn't hike again for ages and I told the rangers on the way out. I phoned them and explained where I was. The saddest thing was that they were used to it."

"It must be hard to forget."

"Yeah." He removed his beanie, scratched at his head and replaced it again. "It is. I think that's why spirits linger, they can't forget either. Want to keep going?"

"Good idea." She almost asked him what he thought about the journal and everything that was going on. But he'd mention it to Kiyomi and that'd only upset her friend. Best to leave it alone. And besides, all the trouble was about to be put to rest.

His boots crunched over leaves until they reached the dip in the earth. She slid after him into the chill hollow, then finally through the treeline and down to Lake Saiko's shore. Daisuke unpacked food at a bench, exchanging a few words with another pair of hikers, but Riko drifted to the water. Fuji loomed in the distance, still big, still grand. The giant that Issa's snail climbed. "A fleshy little engine that could," she murmured.

The lake's surface, a cold sheet of sky, rippled when an insect touched down. Its tiny feet were suction-cup skate-shoes. Never a misstep, little buddy.

"Riko, are you hungry?" Daisuke called. He held up a pair of small packages.

She turned back to the table. "Not really. I wanna get it over with."

"Want me to come?"

"No, thanks. I won't be long."

He held her gaze. "So this was really important, to come out here?"

"It was."

"Kiyomi's pretty worried, you know."

"I know. But it's okay now." Riko said. Everything *was* about to go back to normal. All she had to do was return the journal and she could get on with her life. Find a new job, get things back on track. "It's under control."

"I hope so. I don't like to see you two so stressed."

Riko smiled, took a swig of water, snapped the lid back on and tossed it to him. "Change is coming, Daisuke."

She headed back to the treeline, angling toward the path from where the smoke came last time. Once beneath the trees, she rubbed her arms and stamped her feet to give her circulation a jump start. Cold engines.

An 'x' cut into a tree by a mossy log led her off the trail. She climbed through the undergrowth, detouring ruts in the forest floor, scanning each pale trunk for the marks Kiyomi made last visit, until she came to the spot where she'd fallen. The leaves were still scattered; deep gouges in the soft earth from her hands remained.

She paused, one hand on her shoulder strap.

The suggestion of smoke hung in the air. The clearing? Maybe she should check, just to be sure. It'd only take a moment and surely, if she was being haunted, whatever spirit hounded her wouldn't mind. And if she wasn't, no harm anyway.

She moved on, drawn from marking to marking, each aligned with the scent of smoke, until she stood in the small clearing where the old man had burnt leaves. A black circle stood beneath the canopy, the embers cold. Rake marks had forced the thin grass to lie flat, furrows leading toward the ashes. The scent of smoke was all but gone.

The branches of the oak spread above in a network of smooth brown arms. Odd to see such a tree here. Elsewhere they'd been fir, but the oak stood out. There wasn't a lot of truly level earth in other parts of the forest.

She made a circuit of the tree. Several other piles of faint ash, some greying to white, covered the ground. Many were overgrown. Just how long had he been burning leaves here? And why? She bent by a pile, trailing fingertips through the fine ash. Riko frowned. A tiny metal pin twisted by heat. And beside it, a blackened shell of what must have once been a brooch. Birdsong fell through the leaves. She stood, leaving the brooch in the grey. Maybe he was crazy too.

Time to finish what she came to do. She took the journal from her backpack, the cover cold against her palm, and slipped from the clearing.

At the point where she'd fallen, Riko squatted to dig some more loam away, placing the journal in the earth. "There." She covered it over. "I'm sorry I disturbed you. Please accept my apology, I was wrong. Sleep well, if you will."

Let that be enough.

Daisuke would be waiting. She headed for the narrow trail, tension in her body flowing away, her step lighter. The book was gone. Time to straighten things out. The translation and reading would have to go unfinished. She'd learnt enough. The writer, the woman, had been unhappy. She was caught in a love triangle. Nothing unique, nothing even romantic, but she'd had a dignity. "I liked her," she told the trees.

Back in the clearing, Riko strode to the bench. Daisuke lay across it, hands behind his head, staring up at the sky. He sat when she dumped her bag on the seat. "Hey. All done?"

"All done." She smiled.

"You seem pretty pleased."

"I feel like I can get things on track now."

*

The drive back to Fuji-Yoshida flew by. She laughed and joked, and despite spring rain sloshing down, her spirits were high. What a pallor the threat of more ghostly disruptions had cast upon her. Dealing with her job troubles should have been enough, but even that was not a mountain. It was a hill, steep, but she was a snail. Climbing, slowly, slowly.

She waved Daisuke off and jogged up the drive. Inside, she opened the screen to her bedroom and flung her backpack inside. In the kitchen, Kiyomi stood over the sink, humming to herself as she washed dishes.

Riko paused in the entryway. "Hi."

"Hi. Did everything work out?" Kiyomi's tone was apprehensive.

"All done. I left it where we found it. Daisuke was great."

"Good."

She paused. "Can you still come with me to my appointment? I know you're not too comfortable with that stuff."

Kiyomi spread her arms, soapy water dripping from her hands. "Of course I will."

Riko stepped into the hug, laying her head on her friend's shoulder a moment. "Thanks." It wouldn't hurt to see someone. All she had to do was find a psychiatrist with an open appointment, discuss what happened and then get on with things. *Soldier on* as Mum would say.

"When is it?"

Quick. "Thursday." Two days. The psychiatric community better have someone free. Riko helped Kiyomi put the dishes away, wolfed down a sandwich and slumped into a chair. She rested her cheek on her hand and blinked at the television. It was a game show – contestants hurling themselves at walls while covered in paint – quite odd, especially compared to the 'tame' game shows she knew as a child from Australian TV.

"Riko."

She opened her eyes. "Huh?"

"You're falling asleep."

"Oh." Riko stretched. Her head was heavy and her throat dry. She sipped at a glass of water. "Better go to bed then."

Kiyomi grinned. "Good idea."

Riko showered before stumbling into her room. She kicked her pack aside then climbed onto the bed to check beneath the pillows for spiders, then lay back. Something bright pressed against her eyelids. The lamp, idiot. Rising with a groan, Riko stopped to gape at her backpack.

Fallen on its side, the zip was open and the contents spilled to the floor.

Right beside her drink bottle rested the journal.

Chapter 7

Riko crept over and nudged it with her foot.

The damn thing was real. "No." She snatched the journal, fingers closing on cold leather, and gave it a shake. "Damn you."

Hide it.

Convincing Kiyomi that she was on the mend was hard enough without this. It would undo everything. Riko crammed the journal down into the backpack and dumped it in the bottom of her wardrobe. Good enough for now.

But how the hell had it returned?

She buried it.

Buried. Beneath. Earth.

And here it was, not even dirty! She paced her room. Daisuke wouldn't have touched the journal, let alone slipped it into her bag. And no-one else went with them on the hike. She snorted. "That leaves you, Riko." Ridiculous. Not even a scrap of sense to that. But how to be sure? Could a person block that sort of thing from their consciousness?

Had she really returned it? What if her mind was playing more tricks? Maybe she'd dreamt taking it back? No. That way lay madness. The dirt was real, she'd washed it from beneath her fingernails earlier. She'd been to the forest.

Riko climbed back into bed with a shiver. Even if it killed her – or better than that, knocked her out – she had to sleep somehow. Tomorrow would be a long, long day. She rubbed her socks together to warm her feet. The journal wasn't going to leave her alone. It was like a curse. Maybe she should finally finish reading it. There had to be an answer or a clue in it somewhere, something to help explain what was going on.

She rolled over, reaching for the lamp, then stopped.

Better to leave it on tonight.

*

The Fuji-Yoshida City Library reading room slumbered, dust motes rioting when she slumped into a seat in an out-of-the-way-corner. Her notebook came next, then the journal. A pen followed. Next was a plastic drink bottle.

A large print of Izanagi and Izanami watched over her from the wall. *Searching the Seas with the Tenkei.* They hovered over a mist-shrouded ocean, Izanagi's spear dipping toward the angry waves.

She couldn't stop a shudder.

How powerfully doomed Izanagi's search to rescue his wife from the realm of death.

"Focus," she muttered.

Riko flipped open a page and gripped the pen. *Stop reading.* The message in light across Aunt Eiko's ceiling had been pretty clear. But the journal wasn't going away. And maybe here, the strange light wouldn't find her; it was a public place.

She took a swig of water and shuffled paper, straightening it.

Stop stalling.

Riko peered at the kanji. The first line of a fresh page jumped back in time. The writer recalled her childhood.

> *Mother still wore the Mofuku, the black of her hair was lost in the fabric when she bent to pour tea, but I remember one day, right after Father died, she smiled. I had woven a scarf. She smiled and stroked my head. Was it the last time she truly smiled? I don't know.*

A mourning kimono. Uncommon now perhaps, except with older women. When was the journal written? And who was the writer?

> *our clothesline*
> *taut in the wind*
> *war yet to come*

Another entry mentioning the war. The more Riko translated the more she found. But which war? And then she knew:

> *orange water*
> *the buildings*
> *set to tears*

Firebombing – didn't it have to be the Second World War? She read on until the thumping in her head put a stop to her work. She sculled water and rubbed her temples, slumping back in the chair. What time was it?

She lifted her arm. Noon. Of all the pages that would open, she had only four left – but they were among the more dense in the book. Here the writing became precise, as decisive as she'd seen anywhere else. The final entry she was able to read – there were still more than a few pages stuck together – gave more clues.

> *I am still haunted. Numazu is empty without you. Memory is a powerful poison – and it goes so well with regret. If I have chosen now, finally, I pray that it is right. I must let him go. I have another love, one who is gentle and true, one who deserves all my heart. It cannot beat in so many pieces, I feel like I am hauling around a stone of fire in my chest. You I loved, but my future is here with my husband. I'll still shed a tear for you, the husband I could have had.*

Riko had a location at last. Something else she could add to her notebook but not enough by itself. There had to be more locked within the melded pages. She collected the journal and searched the stacks of packed shelves until she found a librarian reshelving books, trolley at her side.

"Excuse me, can you help me?"

"I hope so." The tall woman placed a couple of volumes aside with a smile.

Riko explained about the journal's condition. "I've tried airing it and I've used my hairdryer, but some of the pages are still stuck together."

The woman nodded. "You could use acid free paper. If

you can insert it between the pages and gently move it like a saw, you should be able to open some more. May I see it?"

Riko handed it over. The librarian flicked through some of the pages, frowning when she hit a thick clump. "Some of these will probably never be readable. But you should be able to get a few apart – I'll bring you the paper. Are you studying here?"

"Yes." Riko thanked the woman. "I'm under Izanagi and Izanami."

"Won't be long." Once the woman returned with several sheets of acid-free paper, Riko got to work. It was slow going, but she was able to free more entries and even cry a small hiss of pleasure when she freed a page stuck to the inside cover. Toward the middle of the page was a name!

Makiko Yamashita.

Riko copied it down so fast it was barely legible. She wrote it again. The name of an older woman – at least now it was. When the journal was written, the writer was hardly an old woman.

So what had happened to Makiko and her mystery man? And what drove her to Aokigahara? The journal wouldn't tell her that easily. Riko stood and walked a short circuit of the reading room, stretching periodically. She'd learned a lot. Most of Makiko's entries – the legible, useful ones anyway – were now noted in her own notebook.

Was it enough to satisfy whatever force sent the journal back? And was it too little to further anger whatever force wanted her to stop reading?

"Excuse me?"

A man in a suit stood before her desk. Instead of a face, he had only a giant moth on the front of his head. Grey mottled wings and blank, black eyes. It twitched.

Riko screamed, falling back.

"Is something wrong?" He leaned closer and she shoved at him, snatching her belongings and stumbling for the door.

"Wait, are you all right?"

Riko tore through the stacks, down the stairs and burst onto the street, panting. The car. Still parked beneath a towering pine tree. Dashing across the road, Riko had the door open, seat belt on and key in the ignition in seconds. She darted out of the park, ignoring a blast of horns, and drove until her apartment building, a grey block with washing stretched across balconies, rose before her.

She killed the engine in the driveway. God, what was happening? Where was his face? And what did moths have to do with anything? Or smoke for that matter? At least this time nothing had leapt in front of her on the drive home.

But the...haunting still didn't make sense – what wanted her to stop and why? All she had was a name, a love triangle and a time period.

Wait. No. She had a city too.

Numazu was only an hour away. Riko nodded to herself. Probably best to try a train, save getting lost. She still wasn't great at navigation when it came to new places. Even back home, she'd get turned around driving in the city.

After the appointment tomorrow, she'd buy a ticket and see if any trace of Makiko could be found. Maybe it was a slim collection of clues for hunting down someone who might not have lived in the sea-side town for decades now, but it had to be worth a shot. It could stop the madness –

and what else did she have to try? If reading the journal caused the haunting and she couldn't get rid of the journal...

The only other option was telling someone everything.

And no-one would believe a word.

Unless she burned the book? No. It'd probably just come back. And she had to know. Why was the journal following her, what was the smoke about? Why her of all people? Was it Makiko, calling her from death?

Riko shuddered. She gathered everything up and rushed to the door. Eyes followed her every step. Or so it seemed. But the street behind her was empty. She opened the door and locked it behind her.

*

The psychiatrist, Dr Kobayashi, adjusted his glasses then shifted in his creaking leather chair. Light from the high window splashed across his immaculate desk, tinting his receding hair. A pen scratched on his notepad while Riko sipped at a glass of water.

"How do you feel, living so far from your family?"

A new line of questioning. She pursed her lips. She'd been honest about her fears, about being haunted, but went in calling them hallucinations – not having to fake concern over their cause at least. He said very little about it, mostly listening. But this was different. "Liberated and isolated."

His deep voice was soft enough that she had to lean forward. "Of course, you're quite far away from them in terms of physical distance. What do you miss?"

"I miss my mother's cooking, her stories. I miss being able to talk to her any time I like."

"And what don't you miss?"

"The pressure. She thinks I should be married by now. She's very traditional and Catholic too."

He made a note on his pad. "And her photo was the first to fall, in your room?"

Back to the ghosts. "Yes."

"What do you think that means?"

"I'm not sure. Do you think I'm responsible but not aware? Like repressed anger or something?"

He leant forward. "Why do you suggest that?"

"Because I don't know what's happening. Can you tell me, can my mind really do things like this?" But she knew, it wasn't her mind. There was no way. The journal was real, she didn't imagine it. And Kiyomi and Daisuke had seen it too.

And yet, she had to ask.

"Certainly. The power of certain delusions can derail lives." He held up a finger. "But I don't think you have to worry about that. Tell me, what about your father? Do you miss him too?"

"Right now, not a lot."

He paused. "I see."

"He's worse than Mum, when it comes to marriage and duty. He didn't even come to the airport to see me off. He was 'sick' and couldn't come."

"You think he wasn't truly sick?"

A long pause. That wasn't fair either. "No, he was. He's always sick. But he didn't want me to go. He thought it was childish; that I was running away."

"Hmmm." More writing. "So, no good memories, nothing positive at all?"

She shrugged. "He introduced me to classic rock."

Now Dr Kobayashi smiled. "That's something." A timer on his desk dinged and an expression of regret passed over his face. "I'm sorry to say that the hour is up. I'd like to see you again, however. Will you make another appointment on the way out? I believe it would be beneficial."

"I will." Maybe. But it would placate Kiyomi at least, who was quietly paying for the appointments, and it hadn't hurt to talk to someone who didn't get angry or upset. But who knew what Dr Kobayashi thought, listening to her describe the haunting?

No matter. It would be a moot point soon enough.

She thanked him and left. Outside, Kiyomi and Daisuke moved forward from the wall they'd been leaning on, sesame ice cream in hand. Kiyomi handed one over and Riko had a mouthful. The warm sun receded just a little at the coolness.

"How was it?" Daisuke shifted on the concrete, cherry blossoms swirling around his feet in a gust of wind.

"The ice cream or the appointment?"

He gave a weak smile but neither he nor Kiyomi laughed at Riko's bad joke. "Maybe we should go to lunch now?" he said.

"If you like," Riko said.

Kiyomi took Riko's hand and squeezed. Riko squeezed back. God, she was a fool to deceive such a good friend. It wasn't just the money – though once her meagre savings ran out, Kiyomi would be paying for pretty much everything else too, petrol, Riko's car park and the insurance, not to mention rent and food – it was the safety of having a friend. Of having someone who would listen, someone who would help no matter what. It was trust.

And Riko knew, she risked losing that too.

She followed them to the car and put on a smile. Just one more night. One more fitful sleep crammed with dreams of her father and of moths, of smoke pouring from Kiyomi's mouth while she juggled white dresses and refrigerators.

Another detail Riko failed to bring up during her session.

One more night and then she'd be on a train to Numazu and whatever answers it held.

Chapter 8

Riko turned into an empty rest stop, pulling her sun visor down for shade and glaring at the GPS screen. "Work, you bastard." She nearly thumped it, but lowered her arm. It was working just fine – the operator was the faulty device.

So much for the 'direct route' to Numazu.

The train station had been almost useless. There was no direct line between Fuji-Yoshida and Numazu. Instead, an eight hour round trip via Tokyo. Which meant she would have struggled to hide the trip from Kiyomi, and so Riko had grabbed a gift card leftover from Christmas and hit the shops.

And now, despite her brand new GPS, she was lost, somewhere outside of Gotenba, on the wrong road. She tapped the screen and zoomed out. There. The Tōmei Expressway –only one of the largest freeways in the whole country and she missed it!

Cars whooshed by on the road beyond. Her stomach rumbled. "Shush," she told it. She'd eat again later. Riko flicked her indicator on and merged with traffic, taking the slow lane and turning up the volume on the GPS.

By driving a little slower and probably irritating other drivers, she found the right exit and had time to switch lanes, passing under a sign for the expressway with a sigh, joining the crowded flow of cars, buses and trucks. Keeping her distance behind a Toshiba truck, she merged again as flashing signs indicated the closing of a lane.

Traffic slowed and she tapped the steering wheel. When it slowed yet further, to half the speed limit, she frowned. The truck blocked her view. What was going on? Checking her mirror, she changed lanes again and groaned.

The expressway was clogged. In the distance, it seemed as if every car was at a standstill. Brake lights flared and she slowed to a crawl, until finally coming to a stop. Had there been an accident? The Toshiba truck rolled to a stop beside her, a red wall. A luxury sedan pulled up beside her, the driver shaking his head. He wound his window down and lit a cigarette. More cars piled up behind her Toyota. Gridlocked. The car in front cut its engine.

Riko followed their example, then paused. "Uh-oh." She gripped the wheel. Something was star-jumping in her stomach. Was it breakfast? She'd only had eggs, nothing unusual.

"Shit."

She flung the door open and leant out as her breakfast splattered across the road in a pale yellow puddle. An acidic burp followed.

She groaned. Where had that come from?

Riko grabbed her water bottle, rinsing her hands and mouth, only to spit when something brushed her hair. She wiped at it, flinching when a moth fluttered to the road. Something else landed in her hair and she brushed it away too, the powder of moth wings coating her fingers when it wouldn't budge. Just how many were...the car ceiling crawled with moths.

Riko tore her seatbelt off and scrambled out of the car with a cry, narrowly missing the vomit. She pressed herself up against the truck, chest heaving as she brushed at her hair. Nothing, and no more moths.

The man from the luxury car called to her. "Are you all right?"

She shook her head.

He got out and walked around the car. "I heard you cry out." He paused when he saw the vomit. "Do you need me to call an ambulance?"

"No, my stomach is just upset." And there was no chance an ambulance would arrive in a hurry anyway. "But could you check something for me?"

"Sure."

"Could you look at my car, inside? I thought there was a massive spider in there."

He smiled. "Of course. Forgive the smell of smoke."

"It's fine."

He ducked in, checking behind the sun visor and a few other places, then pulled his head back. "Sorry, but no sign of any spiders."

"Good." Riko said. Hopefully no moths, either. "Thank you."

He returned to his sedan and Riko stepped over the vomit, lowering herself into the car. No moths. She sighed, part relief, part frustration. Something didn't want her in Numazu.

"I'm still going."

She closed the door to block out the smell of vomit and tried not to move, slumping in the seat. Her stomach still gurgled, but it slowly passed as the afternoon wore on. Other people exited their cars and walked around, some striking up conversations with neighbours while others jumped on their cell phones. By the time traffic started moving, her body was in control of itself again and she was tapping her finger on the wheel.

She didn't look too closely at the accident, just a mess of police and emergency services, and half an hour later, she was driving Numazu's broad streets and heading for the library. And she had to hurry; more than half the day was already gone. The GPS served her well this time, and she pulled up across from the library. The building was a little like an owl with its half-moon roof and two circles like eyes.

She jogged across the road and stepped into the air conditioning. The lobby had a smiling woman who called the archivist. "She'll be here soon."

A smartly dressed woman met her out the front. "Hi, I'm Aya. How can I help?"

"I'm looking for someone actually. It's for a book I'm writing."

"A Numazu resident?"

She nodded. "She would have lived here during the Second World War. Her name was Makiko Yamashita. It's not much, I know."

"Maybe." She smiled. "It's more than some people have when they come to me. Come on, I'll start a search for you."

Riko followed her to a rear office, where she sat across from a desk with a computer. Aya's room was hung with pictures of South America – the ruins of Machu Picchu.

She clicked her mouse and typed a moment before moving the screen around.

"Let's see."

Riko watched the hourglass do its lacklustre dance on the screen. Old computer. It gave a 'bing' and two results appeared. The first was 'Makiko Yamashita', the second a partial match only.

"Okay, that was easy."

"Then she lived here?"

Aya clicked and gestured. "Yes, born here in 1929, worked as a nurse and married a 'Chiba, Saburou' in 1945. After the war she's mentioned just once, in an article about an anniversary of the firebombing. She's pictured placing flowers for someone."

Makiko crouched by a memorial in a dark, flowing kimono. Her long hair was tied into a bun. The sea breeze froze a billowing sleeve and her expression was sombre. Even in her sadness she was lovely and there was a kindness to her face that survived even the black and white archival image on a screen.

So Saburou was Makiko's first love? Was there so much guilt that she later took her life? The picture wasn't the clearest, but Makiko might have been in her thirties. Was she still living in Numazu at that point?

"Could I have a copy of that article?" Riko flipped open her notepad and jotted down the dates onscreen. "Are there any surviving relatives? Children maybe?"

"Hmmm...doesn't look like it."

"What about Saburou's family?"

More clicking and typing. "Here's something. Noriko and Genji Chiba. A niece and nephew by the looks. I've got a picture of Noriko and her family from the Saitama Shimbun but it looks like Genji works for the post office here in Numazu."

"Fantastic. Thank you, I appreciate the help," Riko said as the printer hummed.

Aya smiled as she jotted down some directions on the back of the page, and Riko slipped from the library.

She headed for the post office with its three red lines arranged into a 'T' and jogged up the stairs. Inside she found someone arranging envelopes on shelves and asked about Genji.

"He's actually off work," the woman replied.

Riko gambled. "Oh. I was hoping to see him, I'm his niece. I'm visiting from Saitama."

She smiled. "Oh, you must be Wakako. Genji has mentioned you often."

"Yes." Riko wracked her brain. So close. Another gamble. "Only I'm a bit lost and he's not answering his phone. Has he moved?"

"I'm not sure, I haven't been here that long, but come with me and I'll give you directions. He lives close by. He's probably not answering his phone because he's hurt his leg."

"Thank you, I hope he's okay," Riko said.

"He'll be fine."

Once she had the directions Riko returned to the Toyota and typed them into the GPS. It was close by, and she was soon circling for a parking space before a small house crouching between two bigger homes.

Half a block away, she finally parked, locked up and returned to Genji's house, where she climbed the steps and knocked on the door. Someone called through the wood.

"Sorry, can't come to the door, but it's open."

"Should I come in?"

"Either that or go home, I suppose."

Riko opened the door to an entryway lined with black boots and a pair of slippers. She removed her own shoes and stepped into a neat room hung with family pictures, a smiling man in its centre. His hair was arranged in a careful comb over and he sat with a leg propped up – it was covered in a cast – facing a muted television. A baseball game was on.

"Are you here to deliver my meals? The other girl usually comes later."

"Ah, no. My name is Riko. Are you Chiba-san?"

He nodded. "I'm Genji. What can I do for you?"

"I'm writing a book about women and the war and I wanted to ask about your uncle's wife, Makiko Yamashita."

His face clouded. "A sad tale that one. She used to visit for a while, after Uncle Saburou went missing in the war – at sea they say."

"Did you know her well?"

"Not truly. She was very quiet after that – but there's one thing I can tell you, she always remembered to bring me my favourite sweets."

"She sounds kind."

"She was. I guess that's why she was a nurse. Did you know that?"

"No, thank you for that too. Did she move away?"

"Not long after the navy told her what happened. Maybe only a few months later."

"Do you know where?"

He frowned. "Up north? Could have even been somewhere in Yamanashi."

"Like Fuji-Yoshida?"

He snapped his fingers. "Could be but I'm not sure anymore. Anyway, no-one heard from her much then. I hear she passed away though."

"She did. Well, thank you, Chiba-san."

He stopped her. "Ah, could I ask a favour before you leave?"

"Of course."

He grinned. "Could you make me some tea?"

*

Riko leant her head against her hand as she watched the road, the other hand on the wheel, countryside whipping by. Everything had been easy enough, especially with her fast-talking. She'd stumbled from one helpful person to another – about time she'd had some good luck – but for what? With Saburou lost at sea and Makiko herself dead, that left a general location and Makiko's profession only. And there was little chance that calling every hospital in Yamanashi would yield much.

Yet if Makiko truly did move to Fuji-Yoshida or nearby, that had to help a little. Riko shook her head. But how could she connect Makiko's maiden name to her second husband? If she managed that, maybe then she'd have something. Was the man even still alive? He had to be in the area. That was what the journal wanted her to learn.

Or was it Makiko – pushing her forward?

There was another possibility, another way to cut down the search. If she was willing to take it.

Lake Saiko.

Chapter 9

Riko first wrapped the journal in a plastic bag then a jacket before stowing the bundle beneath a box of old shoes. Next, she slid her washing basket over a little from its usual place and sighed. There. Hidden.

Another shitty night's sleep. Not just because she'd dreamt of moths again, but because she'd woken to throw up. Twice. The second time was mostly dry heaves, nothing left. Still, she blinked as she worked. Shake it off, Riko. You've got a big day today.

Even sick, she was going to put a stop to the haunting.

As far as Kiyomi knew, Riko was visiting Eiko for the night. Instead, it was back to Lake Saiko. And this time at dusk, when the spirit world was said to collide with the human. That way she'd get answers. Know for sure. The few hospitals she'd called had no record of a Makiko Yamashita – but why would they, if she remarried? The search had not been exhaustive, but she had to admit, the trip to Numazu had not taught her enough.

"You're insane, Riko." She didn't stop packing: lots of

water, her phone – charged to the hilt – a torch with spare batteries, a first aid kit, food, compass and map. And a pocket knife. And the journal. One more thing and she was set.

An omamori from Fuji-Yoshida Sengen Shrine.

Sengen Shrine lay north of Lake Saiko but what better place to find a charm for protection, than a shrine dedicated to the Shinto deity of Mt Fuji?

In the kitchen she boiled water and tapped her fingers on the bench top. With each movement her stomach lurched. Too bad. No time to be sick. She just had to solider on. Riko spooned coffee into a mug and poured the water after it. Probably wouldn't do the old stomach any good, but better than a crash.

Bitter black. She put the mug down to load the Toyota's cramped boot, letting the coffee cool. When she was done, she had a few more sips and left it unfinished. It was strong enough. Locking up, Riko jumped into her car and hit the road.

She drove north, and not long out of the city the highway started to curve toward the mountain. She sipped at one of her water bottles. Her stomach had settled some, but the discomfort was replaced with a headache. She switched off the radio – silencing an announcer's promises, and switched on the GPS. Following it's instructions, it wasn't too long before the exit for Sengen Shrine appeared.

Her lids were heavy. "No." She had to be alert, in case something jumped in front of the car again. Riko wound down the window and the roar of cold air straightened her in the seat. Switching the radio back on, loud, helped too. Girls Generation blasted an earnest love song, which she soon flicked off, but it worked. When she pulled up to the shrine's car park, it was with a surging pulse. Would the Shinto priests let her have an omamori? What was the process exactly? Maybe there'd be a gift shop.

A misty rain fell at the shrine, light on Riko's cheeks as she joined the flow of visitors. She trailed a tour group and a pair overburdened by hiking gear, walking beside a girl who nodded on her phone. Lined by rounded stone lanterns and massive, sentry-like cedars, the path was a long corridor.

A huge torii rested before the shrine, the wooden gate a slick red in the mist. She passed beneath it and skirted the main hall, moving toward one of the other buildings where hangings at a service window advertised a gift shop.

A man smiled at her when she approached. "How can I help you? An omikuji perhaps, to tell your fortune?"

"Uh, I'm looking for an omamori."

"Certainly. We have many kinds, including key chains. Hello Kitty perhaps? You are studying?"

Riko hesitated. Hello Kitty going up against an increasingly angry spirit didn't seem like enough firepower. "I've never had one before. I was hoping for a strong one." She met his gaze and held it.

He nodded. "Something more traditional, perhaps." He rummaged around and brought over a small cloth bag of purple with hand-stitched kanji. She had to squint to read it. Sengen Shrine. On the other side, a ward against evil.

"Keep it with you. Don't open it and after a year, bring it back for cleansing. You must never throw it away, it will anger the deity."

"Thank you." She paid him and put the amulet in her jeans pocket, wandering back down the corridor of cedars whose green needles were beaded with water. She breathed deep; the air was so clean.

Yet one of the hikers had already begun to sneeze, probably hay fever from lingering pollen. After the war, the government had planted too many cedar trees, hoping to benefit from cheap, local timber. Apparently it caused near epidemic allergies. Riko hadn't believed it when she first arrived in Japan, but Kiyomi had shown her a newspaper report and the money spent on trying to control the allergies was serious.

She slowed, adjusting her backpack. Going back to Aokigahara was probably a mistake. A life-scarring kind of mistake. But what was the alternative? Stick around, looking for work while moths, smoke and ghosts overtook her life? Or ran her off the road?

The Toyota was covered in dew, rivulets ran down the driver's window when she swung the door open and hopped in. She hit the wipers and pulled out of the car park then back onto the highway. Riko put her foot down. "Come on."

By the time she reached the entrance to the forest, the rain was gone. Only a cold sky of rumpled steel watched over her as she started up the damp trail. Aokigahara loomed, the dark green of the trees and the mutated land rising and falling around the trail. Her breathing grew loud in the hush. Kiyomi's warning echoed. If she left the trail, what would she find? Skeletons, sinking into the moss? Her foot caught on a fallen branch. Concentrate, idiot.

She trudged on, slipping on wet leaves often enough that her hands were slick with mud by the time she reached the lake's quiet edge. She bent by the water and washed the dirt and leaves away, Fuji's reflection rippling beyond.

As was becoming tradition, she ate on a bench – plain

biscuits only – as the light faded before heading back into the forest, and again, followed Kiyomi's markings on trees until she reached the spot where she'd left the journal – before it followed her home anyway. She nudged the loose dirt, just to be sure. No journal. Where to wait?

The forest was poised.

A single leaf fluttered to the ground, soundless.

Somewhere open – the oak. If the spirits could find her in Fuji-Yoshida, they could manage to find her by the oak too. She hurried on, reaching the clearing and removing her pack.

"Here I am, then," she muttered. Only silence from the forest, and she shivered as she rested against the trunk. Next she pulled out her torch and water then patted the omamori in her pocket. Time passed and darkness crept. The trunks around her grew pale in the failing light, but the spaces between them were voids. Something wet hit her head; a drop of water from the leaves. She raised her plastic raincoat hood.

The night wore on with the occasional drop of water hitting her coat.

She shivered. She shifted her legs, sipped from her water, snacked on dry biscuits. "Where are you then?"

Dusk had passed. The spirit world, if it even existed, if she wasn't insane, was supposed to be closest at dusk. And she'd sat beneath a tree in the middle of a haunted forest in the dark and nothing.

"Come on. I don't want to go home and find more crazy shit, please. Tell me what you want?"

Only the dark. She stood. How much rubbish was she supposed to put up with then? How long until the ghosts or spirits gave her peace?

"Hey!" she snapped. "Show up or piss off."

More silence.

Riko burst into laughter. When had she become such an idiot? Staying in a forest at night waiting for ghosts to appear? Worse, endangering her own life – what if she got lost heading back? Eventually starved to death?

A chill ran across her body. Her fingertips were like buttons of ice.

She jammed her supplies into the backpack, checked the extra batteries and flicked the torch on. The beam tore through the shadows. The raked grass and patches of ash were bright and the tree trunks pale. She squinted at each one, running the torch up and down. Kiyomi's marks were thin in the light.

Her skin prickled, as if eyes followed her. She clenched her teeth. There was nothing there, she was being stupid.

Still, Riko spun, light flashing. She checked between every tree but the limit of the light revealed only shadows. How vast the forest. If she was turned around, if there *was* something out there with dark intent, man or spirit, she could be lost and never found.

She fought a tremble as she moved on, checking the ground every few steps, avoiding snags as she followed scuff marks from her arrival. Twice it took her a full examination of a tree to find the mark. And then no tree anywhere nearby had a mark – and there was no clearing or main path. She backtracked, moving to some fresh trees. Her breath steamed, disappearing when it passed out of the beam of light.

Something rustled in the distance and she froze.

Don't panic. Riko sucked in a deep breath through her nose. Just find the last mark and go from there. Her foot falls squelched in the night as she approached another tree. The bark was cold beneath her palm. No markings. Riko bit into her lip. "Shit."

A clicking echoed in the wood. She spun again, whirling the torch. Trees flashed. The clicking returned, still in the dark, echoing. As if two stones were being knocked together in an off-rhythm.

"Who's there?" She slung the pack around and rummaged for the pocket-knife. The blade seemed pitifully small. The clicking stopped. Riko put her back to a tree, chest heaving. "Well? Where are you?"

The clicking resumed. She raised the blade, arm shaking. Closer still came the odd clicking and then a shape formed out of darkness. It hulked between the trunks, massive shoulders hunched over a white face. Black hair fell to the ground, pooling at its feet. Closed eyes regarded her, the mouth painted in a black frown. It stepped over a log, the white linen of its kimono rustling. The clicking became apparent – a string of skulls hung from its neck. Human, bird, fox, rabbit, even mice, all clicked as it moved. A faint glow swam beneath the dark eye-lids.

Shinigami - death-spirit.

She lifted her chin, trembling as its face angled down. Still the eyes were closed. A hand lifted, dirt trailing between the fingers. It paused before her, open, entreating. Dirt continued to flow, tiny clouds stirring on the ground. Her knife faltered. The closed eyes followed her hand, a great sadness pouring forth. The head titled, as if a question. Was it asking her...the spirit wanted to know, did she wish for death? Had she come to Aokigahara to die?

Riko shook her head.

The spirit turned away, skulls clinking as a lock of its hair brushed her hand. She gasped as the forest dimmed and the ground rose with a slowness unnatural. She hit, and the leaves swallowed her, warm and forgiving.

*

"Hey, wake up." A hand shook her shoulder.

Riko groaned.

"This one's alive." The first voice.

"Good." A second voice.

Someone patted her cheek. "Come on, young lady. Come on."

Were her eyes glued together? She stretched her leg, folded beneath her. Leaves crunched. The death-spirit! She flinched, raising her hands. Someone caught them.

"It's all right, you're safe."

Light burst through cracks in her eyelids. Green came into focus, then a worried face. A middle aged man knelt over her. The characters: 'Fuji-Hakone-Izu National Park' were clear on his jacket, his beanie embroidered with the same kanji. His first name was printed too. 'Akio'.

"Are you all right, are you hurt?" He helped her sit. The other ranger, an older man, scrutinised her from a short distance away. "Glad you didn't do it, girl. Hate finding the young women like you."

Akio merely looked at her.

"I didn't come here for that," she said. "I was hiking to Saiko and I got lost."

"And you slept here?" The second man's tone suggested that he didn't find her all that credible.

Riko frowned at him. "Yes. I didn't want to get any more lost, it was too dark. I thought I had a better chance of finding my way back in daylight."

He glared. "So why did you leave the path in the first place?"

Akio held up a hand. "That's enough, Tetsu." He turned back to her. "Now young lady, don't worry. You're not far from Saiko, you were quite close. You did the right thing by camping out, though my grumpy friend is right. You shouldn't leave the trail. You're lucky we found you."

"I thought I smelt smoke," Riko said. Explaining herself to Akio was easier than Tetsu. Even with a lie.

Akio exchanged a look with his companion.

"What?"

Tetsu shrugged. "That'd be Hiroshi. Burning his dead wife's clothes. Crazy old fool."

"He has a tree nearby," Akio said. "And he's been burning his wife's possessions under it for decades. No-one knows why. Most people avoid him."

Tetsu crossed his arms. "So they should. The crazy fool has attacked hikers with that bloody rake of his."

"He hasn't attacked them. He threatened a couple once."

"It's happened more than once."

Akio threw up his hands. "Well it doesn't matter does it?" He shook his head but smiled at Riko, his eyes crinkling. "We'll take you back to the Lake now."

"Thank you." Riko collected her pack and followed the two rangers to the trail. Warm light filtered through the trees. "Did his wife die here? Hiroshi?"

"Yes. Long ago I'd guess."

Riko hesitated. If she seemed too interested, they'd go back to thinking she was crazy. But what if? It had to be Makiko – to hell with coincidence. "What was her name?"

"No idea," Akio said, eyes busy with the trail ahead. Tetsu gave her a look but said nothing.

The sun was high in the sky when they exited the forest, its rays banishing the chill. Across the clearing were two small groups cooking with a portable hotplate. She lifted her face a moment. The smell of fried fish drifted over. Her stomach rumbled. "It's always beautiful," she said, turning to Fuji.

Akio smiled. "Are you confident from here?"

"Yes. Thank you both."

Tetsu grunted, but gave her a nod. "Just be safe, all right?"

"I will." She looked to Akio. "About Hiroshi, does he live nearby?"

Even Akio frowned this time. "Near enough. Why would you ask?"

"Well, back home I'm a counsellor, I thought maybe –"

"No." Tetsu shook his head. "He won't go for that. Just have something to eat and head home, young lady."

"All right, thank you again." She waved them off then sat on 'her' bench and unpacked ham sandwiches and obento – rice balls. She chewed. Each bite was a slow avalanche – the food tasted stale and she didn't finish the ham. Her hand tingled where the death-spirit's hair brushed it. If even that much contact put her to sleep, then taking its hand...Riko shuddered.

Instead of finding Makiko, she'd found the woman's husband after all. That had to be who Hiroshi was. Why else all the smoke – a signal, leading her back there? How old must Hiroshi be by now? And would he believe her claims of haunting? More. Could he even do anything to help her? Maybe he'd lost the journal? No matter what, she had to speak with him. Riko took another bite then stopped – the obento halfway to her mouth.

Her stomach flipped and she jumped up, managing only two steps before heaving her lunch onto the grass. She spat bile and went for her second water bottle, rinsing her mouth and searching the bag for a tissue. Finding none, she tried her pockets and stopped when her fingers met the omamori.

She drew it out. The wooden prayer within the woven bag was broken.

Chapter 10

Riko threw up again before she reached her car. This time the dry heaves sent her to her knees and her throat tore on each hack. Tears streamed down her cheeks. She drank the rest of her water, the cool soothing her throat. Before she could stand she'd coughed it up again.

What was happening? Did she get sick overnight? There was no reason, aside from stress, for it to happen now. Unless the rice was bad. Or it was some sort of bug. If so, any time she ate she was in for more of the same.

She could hold out for a doctor then. All she had to do was drive home. Her nose wrinkled; and shower. Riko fumbled with the keys. She spat more bile before changing her hiking shoes for runners and getting into the car to pull out of the park. The highway was busy but she was home before Kiyomi left for her shift at the library.

"Riko!" Kiyomi, dressed in her smart blue University Library uniform, rushed down the drive as Riko got out of the car. "Are you all right? Where have you been?"

"Yeah, I'm fine." Was the hiking pack in the back seat or the boot? If Kiyomi saw it…"What's wrong?" Riko tried to position herself in front of the window.

"You've been gone for days."

Riko gave her friend a look. "Days?"

"Your phone's been out of service and Eiko had no idea where you were." Her relief faded and her voice hardened. "Damn it, Riko. We were afraid. I even rang your mother."

"Kiyomi, I've only been away overnight."

"No, you haven't. It's Monday."

"It's Friday afternoon."

She held up her iPhone. Monday the Eleventh of April. Riko snatched the phone. "This has to be wrong."

Kiyomi took it back. "It's not. So where were you? Your aunt says you never visited." Her lips were compressed into a line.

Riko opened her mouth but gave up. Kiyomi wouldn't believe the truth, wouldn't want to listen. It would only upset her. And her friend deserved something better than a lie that would only unravel later. Keep it simple. "I don't know."

Kiyomi said nothing.

Riko leaned against the Toyota. "I thought I went to Aunt Eiko's."

"You didn't."

Riko looked away, near to choking. Bile rose up her throat and she retched. No vomit splashed onto her shoes, but she grasped for the car.

Kiyomi reached out. "What have you done to yourself?"

"It's been happening for days," Riko gasped between

retches and coughing. "Water."

Kiyomi led her inside, taking her straight to the kitchen. "My shoes."

"Don't worry about it now."

Riko gripped the bench as her stomach twisted. The pain leapt beyond 'useful distraction' to trembling agony.

"You're all white." Kiyomi handed a cup over.

Riko drank and the water charged back up her throat, splashing into the sink. She slid down against the bench. "I think –" Riko groaned, rolling onto her side and pulling her knees up to her chest.

"I'm calling an ambulance," Kiyomi shouted.

Riko clenched her teeth, the scrambling form of Kiyomi a distant blue blur. Tears built. Something was wrong – what a stupid thought! Writhing on the floor didn't mean peaches.

The pain passed.

"...yes, yes, I need an ambulance," Kiyomi was saying from above.

"Wait, it's stopped."

"Sorry." Kiyomi loomed over her, phone in hand. "Are you sure?"

Riko nodded, the air cool on her cheeks. Kiyomi made her apologies to the emergency services.

It wasn't the death-spirit. She'd been vomiting before. And she hadn't eaten again since waking in the forest. No. It was what the ghost wanted, whoever was trying to stop her. They wanted her sick and unstable. And it wasn't Makiko. If anything, Makiko was sending the smoke – someone else was sending moths and stomach cramps.

Kiyomi knelt to stroke her hair. Riko smiled up at her, a bead of sweat trickling down her temple and neck. "I'll see someone about this. I must have a bug."

"You better."

Riko closed her eyes. Another lie. Keep it going, while Kiyomi was vulnerable. "I must be crazy if I can't remember where I've been for days."

"We'll help you, me and Daisuke, your aunt. Even your parents."

"How was Mum?"

"About twenty seconds away from a plane ride."

"Yeah?" Nice to know – but Dad? Bet he'd barely stirred from the couch. Or hospital bed. No, that was too much. Being a bitch seemed to go hand in hand with lying.

"Of course. I told her that the police had everything under control, and that I'd call her every hour with updates."

God, the police. That'd be trouble. "I guess I should call her now."

"Rest a bit first," Kiyomi said as she rose. "I'll call the police. Can you stand?"

"I think so."

Kiyomi dealt with Riko's shoes and then helped her up and over to the couch. Riko lay back, counting between breaths and resting the cool glass against her forehead. The dark television screen was featureless – perfect.

Kiyomi eventually returned, a steaming bowl of miso soup in her hand. "Here."

Riko accepted it. "Thank you." She sniffed, tears stinging her eyes. God, Kiyomi would be so hurt if she knew how much Riko was lying. But it was madness. She wouldn't believe a word. Keep lying, Riko – it's the only way. Tomorrow, she could figure out how to sort the mess she'd made and find Hiroshi.

"Sorry, Riko. I didn't think. Will you be able to keep it down?"

"I have no idea." She inhaled. Onion and shrimp. Delicious. And yet…"Maybe you should eat it. I'm sorry Kiyomi. It's better in the bowl than all over my shirt and your couch." Riko put the bowl aside and leant her head back.

"Maybe you should get an early night?" Kiyomi suggested. "I can call Dai-kun and see if he'll take you to the doctor tomorrow?"

"That's a good idea, thanks." Better than the hospital. She smiled at Kiyomi on her way to the bedroom and her desk, where she took out her phone and dialled home.

It rang out. She dialled her mother's mobile.

"Riko, thank God, where have you been?" Her mother's voice seemed to crack the tiny phone speakers.

"I'm all right, Mum."

"We've been worrying for days, do you hear me? Days."

Riko sighed, but with a smile.

"Don't you give me that, young lady."

"No, Mum, it's just good to hear your voice. Even when you're angry with me." Her own voice wavered. Clenching her muscles, holding her nerve and chewing all the lies and half-truths was a good shield. It kept the fear at bay. And she was in trouble. Even without the vomiting, the spirits, her job, her friendship with Kiyomi, everything balanced on a pin's head.

"A sniff came across the phone line. "Oh sweetheart, you're in trouble, aren't you?"

"I am."

"We tried to call. After we heard from Kiyomi."

"I know. My phone was flat." Back to lies, but small ones,

and hopefully not for long. "I lost track of some days, Mum. It's like I blacked out." Not exactly a lie.

"Have you been to the hospital, then?"

"We're going to run some tests. See if they can find anything."

"Did you hit your head then?"

"I must have. It's scary."

"I'm packing my bags, Riko."

"No, it's okay. I have Kiyomi and Aunt Eiko, I'll be okay. We have a good hospital here; it's fine. But I'm glad you're here now."

"But I'm not there, darling."

"You know what I mean. It's good to talk." Riko shifted to the bed, sitting on its foot. "How's Dad?"

"He's home again. And he's worried about you."

"Is he there?"

"He's sleeping. The operation was hard on him. But I'll get him to call you tomorrow. You won't be at work, will you?"

"No. But that'd be good." He wouldn't call, so she had to ask. "Operation?"

"His back again, but it looks good. They think this will be the last time for a few months."

"Good."

Her mother paused. "Now, are you sure you don't want me to come and visit?"

"It's too expensive, Mum. Not with Dad sick."

"We'd find a way."

"I'm fine. And I'm going to hospital tomorrow. I'll tell you how it went, okay?"

"All right. Get some rest then. I'll call you tomorrow."

Riko said goodbye and hung up, rang her aunt to let her know she was fine, then lay back on the bed, fully clothed. She rolled over and forced herself to check for spiders then gave a sigh. Everything else could wait until tomorrow.

The pillow was a cloud.

*

The police never showed up, thankfully, and so she went straight to a doctor's clinic the next morning – only marginally preferable to a hospital. She tapped her foot in the white waiting room and the x-ray machine brought pictures of Dad, his own face pale and tight with pain, rushing back.

She squashed them down.

In the doctor's office she tried to relax in the squeaky chair while he looked over the results. The doctor's shaven hair had a patch of white in the black, and he shook his head as he looked over the results. "Nothing shows up on the x-rays," he said. "It looks clear."

"Good," Riko said. But he wasn't going to find anything to explain what happened. Maybe a Witch Doctor was what she needed.

"I think you should go to the hospital for a CAT scan, just to be sure." He scribbled at a pad. "Here's a referral, hopefully they can book you in soon. We'll know more once the blood tests are in too."

"Thank you, Doctor. I hope so." She accepted the piece of paper. Hopefully it would placate the others enough to get everything sorted.

Outside, a light rain spotted Daisuke's old Beach Boys

jacket where he waited for her and he raised his eyebrows when she approached.

"He couldn't find anything." The folded referral was suddenly burning a hole in her pocket. She didn't have to go; there was nothing wrong with her. Not like that, anyway.

"Really?" He ran a hand through his bleached hair. "That's not good."

"Maybe. There's more results still coming." She shrugged. "But I haven't eaten today and I haven't thrown up either."

"That's something I guess."

They walked to the car in silence, and when he got in, Daisuke didn't start the engine. He watched the traffic. It hummed by. Somewhere a car alarm squealed.

"Daisuke?"

He sighed, fiddling with the keys. "Ah, Riko, this is hard to say."

She waited.

"Me and Kiyomi, we're still worried about you."

"I know. I'm sorry. I know you're both concerned."

He nodded. "It's like you're not really 'together' lately. Ever since you lost your job, you know?"

"I know."

"And that journal, you know how crazy it's made you act?" He couldn't look at her very long before glancing away again.

"Yeah." Where was he going? Poor Daisuke, must have been hard for him.

"Well, maybe you shouldn't go back to Lake Saiko. Just to be sure, you don't, you know, relapse? Returning the journal was the right thing to do by the spirits I think." He smiled. "When we were there you seemed really driven, it was good, even though I was expecting you to ask me to come with you for the last bit. You're hopeless with directions."

Riko took his hand. "I'm doing better now, Daisuke. I might have to go back one day. Who knows? But I'm not worried about that now. I want to figure out what's wrong with me." Yet more lies. And they were getting pretty bloody heavy. Her shoulders twitched.

"Me too." He started the car and they drove in silence until he dropped her off.

"Are you coming over tonight?"

"Tomorrow," he said. "Kiyomi's having dinner with her parents tonight."

"See you then, then."

He waved as he drove off. Riko stood before the apartment building and looked to the distant shape of Fuji, a purple giant on the horizon, cloud brushing its face. Somewhere at his feet Hiroshi roamed. She had to find the old man and get the truth. Even if she had to wrestle it from him and his rake.

Chapter 11

She kept every light in the apartment on while Kiyomi was out.

But no ghosts came.

In the cool of the night, the TV murmuring from the other room, she prepared her hiking gear again, adding extra water and food to her stores – though why she bothered with the food… All she'd done was sip at water for two days now, and no throwing up. She wasn't game to eat yet, but her stomach ached with emptiness. Twice she stopped, just to sit still and imagine dumplings lounging in sauce. Or pizza back home.

Finally, she unpacked the journal from its hiding place and stowed it in the bottom of her pack. Tomorrow Hiroshi would read it and prove that he knew Makiko. Her only problem was finding him. Camping out at his tree, even during the day, wasn't much of an option. Even Akio and Tetsu didn't know when Hiroshi would appear. She would have to find his home.

Her phone rang from the dresser. Caller unknown. She hit answer. "Hello?"

"Can you meet me outside?"

"Who's this?"

"Yuuki Ikeda."

She ran to the front window. "Where are you?"

"By the big tree."

Riko hung up. She rushed to the front door and stepped into the dark. There. Beneath the tree, Yuuki paced, hands in pockets. He was mostly silhouette, back-lit by the streetlight.

She stormed over, concrete cold beneath her socks. "Yuuki, what are you doing here? Do you want to get me sent back to Australia?"

Yuuki flinched. "No, I came to warn you. Dad's been talking about you a lot."

A chill wormed its way through her bones. "What's he saying?"

"That maybe he shouldn't have let you off the hook for what you did."

She jabbed her finger at him. "For what you did."

"I'm sorry! He'll kill me if I tell him I lied."

She shook her head. "Go home, Yuuki."

"But I had to come here."

"Why, Yuuki? You're not going to tell the truth, so why bother?"

He stepped back and light fell upon his face. A bruise covered his cheek and eye, the swelling enough to distort his face. Riko gasped.

"I have to warn you. He's...not like my dad anymore. He was always strict, but now he's worse."

"Yuuki, what happened?"

The young man became jittery. "I thought it would help you if I came. He's talking to someone at the Immigration

Bureau next week. Please, Riko-san, don't hate me."

He opened his mouth, as if to add more, then turned and ran. He flashed through the next pool of light but did not look back.

"Wait." Riko looked to the pitiful stars above. "Just what I need."

*

Kiyomi knocked on her door. "Are you up yet, Riko?"

"Yeah." She frowned at the clock; its black face blinked. Had the power gone out last night? "What time is it?" Light filled the hallway. "Time for uni already?"

"You slept in. It's two." She spoke through the door. "Another meeting with my supervisor before my shift."

"Is everything okay?"

"I'm a bit behind on a deadline is all. What about you, are you all right?"

"I think so. Come in and sit down."

Kiyomi opened the door. Her outfit was precise, matching grey and blue. Riko patted the bed. When Kiyomi sat, the familiar scent of orange slipped from her hair. "Do you feel sick?" she asked.

"No. Not yet anyway."

"Good." Kiyomi hesitated. "So, what are your plans today?"

"I'm going to a Shinto Shrine and then I'll book an appointment at the hospital. I want them to do some tests." One half-truth and one lie. Both bitter on her lips.

"Really? A shrine? I didn't think you were religious."

"Maybe I should be."

"All right, well...we'll see you tonight." She stood then

paused at the door. "Do you think it's safe for you to drive?"

"I hope so. If I feel funny, I'll take a taxi."

Kiyomi nodded. "Do you need some money?"

"No, thanks though."

"All right, see you tonight."

Riko waited for Kiyomi's car to leave then sprang out of bed. A wave of dizziness set the room to spinning and she stumbled against the dresser. Growling, she cleaned up and dressed before eating a KitKat over the sink. Green tea – Kiyomi's favourite flavour, and a little strange, but Riko was used to them now.

She waited.

Her stomach rumbled but nothing happened. She took another drink and tapped her foot to the tune of Deep Purple's *Smoke on the Water*. A favourite song her father played often when she was little. Thanks for that, at least, Dad.

She stuffed napkins into her pockets, checking on the omamori before dialling for directory. It had protected her once; would even a broken omamori be better than nothing?

"Fuji-Hakone-Izu National Park please," she said when the operator picked up.

"Connecting you now."

Beeps and clicks. The line connected. "Hakone National Park, Izumi speaking."

"Hi, my name is Riko Nakamura and I'm trying to find someone."

"In our offices?"

"Well, maybe. Could I speak with someone who is familiar with Lake Saiko?"

"Regarding?"

"There's a man who rakes leaves there and I don't know how to find him."

Izumi laughed. "Oh, him. Everyone knows Hiroshi Miyamoto. We've passed on complaints about him to the police before, he's a touchy guy."

"Great, so do you think I could have his phone number? I'm trying to interview him for a book I'm writing."

"He doesn't have a phone."

"Would anyone know his address? Akio perhaps?"

"You know Akio Kimura?"

"Not really. But he helped me hiking one day."

"Well he'd know. I'll have to call you back, he's out."

"Fantastic." Riko gave her mobile to Izumi and waited. Maybe it was stupid – but she'd been doing stupid things for days now. And she couldn't just sit home and do nothing. The time to hesitate was well past. She walked to the kitchen and took a drink of water, tapping her finger. She switched on the television but turned it off.

"Come on, Akio." Kiyomi wouldn't be gone all day.

Maybe the journal would have something else to say? There were a few pages she hadn't read yet...

On the kitchen table Riko spread the journal and her acid free paper, supporting its covers with two other books, wincing when the spine creaked. Despite her efforts to dry the pages, the musty scent of the forest lurked in the paper.

Slowly, she sawed between two pages.

Bon Festival

People took their warm lanterns down to the sea, the yellow glow giving the buildings a beauty beyond

> *their brick and eaves, hiding scars from the war. You*
> *surprised me that night, you promised me 'forever'*
> *and you seemed to believe it possible. And in a shiver*
> *that slipped between a sudden hush in the crowd, I*
> *was sure our ancestors heard.*

And on the next page, this one seemed to be a different day

> *You tried to comfort me but there was something*
> *stronger than either of us. Despicable. There is*
> *nothing it cannot steal meaning from.*

No real clues. Riko stood to stretch her legs, pacing with her mobile in hand. Where was he? "Hurry up, Akio."

As if on cue, her phone rang.

"Hello, Riko speaking."

"Yes, this is Akio. You're the girl we found near Saiko? Are you all right?"

"I am, and thank you again."

"Izumi told me you wanted to visit Hiroshi Miyamoto? I'm not sure it's a good idea."

Riko hesitated. Should she mention Makiko's journal? Or perhaps a story about being interested in speaking to him? An interview perhaps – a journalist? "I'm hoping to speak to him about his life. I'm writing a book and I'm researching the history of the Fuji Five Lakes."

"A writer and a counsellor, huh?"

She forced a laugh. "Everyone's got to have a hobby."

"Certainly."

"I think he'd be a great subject, he'd have quite a story to tell, don't you think?"

"I don't doubt it, but I don't know how he'd react."

She improvised. "I'll be taking my boyfriend with me."

"Well..."

"It would save us some time, otherwise we'll have to check all the surrounding villages."

He sighed. "All right. Just take care, I'd hate to hear of you getting hurt."

"I will." She scribbled down the address, thanked him, gathered her things and jumped into the Toyota, heading for a petrol station. Finally, some real progress!

Traffic in streets and on the highway was busy, but she only had half an eye on it. The other was on her GPS. Hiroshi wouldn't be too hard to find – the village of Narusawa, maybe twenty minutes away, but she couldn't afford to get lost this time and she'd already had one delay.

"Not too much to ask, is it?"

No-one answered.

Riko drove, following the instructions issued in the cheerful voice, her movements becoming automatic. Turn left. Go straight. Turn right. The roads gradually became less maintained, until she was bumping along a dirt road with potholes, the trees rising up on either side.

"Turn left in ten metres, destination is fifty metres on the left."

She eased the car up a curving driveway, concealed by a stand of cedar trees and stopped at the front door. Hiroshi's house had a Meiji-era influence with its tiled roof, eaves tilted up. It was small but still grand-looking. Old but not run down, with clean windows and a swept path.

Akio's and Tetsu's description of the old man chasing

people away with a steel rake was hard to shrug off as she crunched over the dirt and gravel, coming to a halt at his door. She rapped on the smooth wood and stepped back. All she had to do was mention Makiko as soon as possible. Then he'd want to talk.

No answer. She moved to a window and peered inside. A low divan sat across from a blocky television, a small table with a clear surface sat on tatami mats. Even through the window the mats appeared spotless.

But a photo atop the television caught her eye.

A couple stood before the house, standing close but not touching. Hiroshi and Makiko. His hair wasn't as wild and it was dark, and Makiko's face was unlined. An unlit candle rested before the photo.

"Hello? Hiroshi-san?"

Still nothing. Riko circled the house, passing an old bicycle leaning against the side of the building. Missing a chain, it was the closest thing to untidy, and yet – even the pedals were level and the seat free of fallen leaves. The stone walkway too, looked as if it had just been swept. Needles and leaves from cedar and oaks spread across the crew-cut grass, but not a single one on the stone.

The rear garden stretched to a distant fence, dotted with hedges, plants and three water features. In one, a lithe fox had curled its tail but no water spouted from its mouth. An empty space before an open shed, with old grooves where wheels would rest, must have usually housed a car. Was he even home? Riko shook her head. Idiot. He was probably at the Lake.

She moved to the shed just in case, peering around the door.

A skylight beamed down onto a spotless concrete floor, a workspace where tools lined the walls and a vice stood bolted to one of the benches, but no Hiroshi. Yet standing just beyond the stripe of light was a dark jumble of shapes.

She crept forward, bending down.

Riko gasped.

The dark jumble was made up of dozens of carvings – each of a woman. Some were the length of her palm, others tall as a water bottle and many, mostly unfinished, could have been a statue on one of the fountains or even something resting in the entryway to a house. There had to be dozens.

She picked one up and moved into the light. The woman wore a kimono and the back of her hair was tied into a neat bun, the texture of her hair indicated by feather-light markings, and her face...

Makiko.

The carving wore a small smile but the eyes were unfinished, blank. Riko shivered. Had he carved them all as a replacement, a reminder?

An engine, grumbling up the driveway.

Riko jumped, dropping the carving. It clunked on the ground and she nudged it back to the heap with her foot before dashing around the house to stand by her car. An old blue truck, with rounded wheel wells and cabin, rattled up the drive. Inside, a man with a sheet of white hair stared at her, eyebrows drawn. He screeched to a halt beside the Toyota and jumped out of his truck, slamming the door.

"What do you want?"

Riko raised her hands. She had to be sure he was actually Hiroshi. "I'm looking for Hiroshi Miyamoto."

He came to tower over her. "Doesn't live here. Now, off

you go. No visitors."

"But it's about Makiko Yamashita."

His face froze, as if she'd punched through an ancient wall, shattering his heart. Then he leant down. His voice dropped. "I said 'go'."

"Please, I think I have her –"

The old man roared, an animal cry, and Riko fell back, bumping into her car.

"I said 'go', did you hear me? Now." Hiroshi stretched for a shovel where it stood in a garden bed.

Riko scrambled round the Toyota and tore the door open. Glass shattered and a thump rocked the car – he'd smashed her tail light. She stomped on the pedal as another smash came, flinging dust into Hiroshi's face as she sped off.

In the mirror, he was coughing and spluttering, half-bent, shovel in hand.

Chapter 12

On the way home she stopped for a meal in a quiet cafe, eating a plain noodle dish and beaming when she kept it down. The waitress probably thought she was crazy, grinning at an empty cup.

The sky was darkening into a deep blue when Riko pulled up to her driveway, blocked from entering by a familiar black Lexus. A young man leant against the hood in a smart outfit but no hat this time, with legs crossed and a cigarette in hand. Konda exhaled a plume of white smoke when she approached.

"She's here, Shachō." His voice was tight. Was he afraid?

Her stomach flipped. What had Yuuki done now? Did Ikeda know out about his son's last visit? "Why does Ikeda-san want to see me?"

Konda only dropped his cigarette and squashed it with his dress shoe.

"Konda?"

The rear door snapped open and Ikeda slipped from the car in one motion. His suit was impeccable once again and he did not smile. A new light filled his eyes; their colour had even lightened since she last saw him. Contacts? He didn't strike her as vain. Stern, yes, but not vain.

Ikeda raised an eyebrow. "I've been waiting for some time now, Riko-san. Konda?" He nodded to the driver, who leapt forward and caught her shoulders. Cigarette-breath was heavy on her face.

"Hey!"

Ikeda waved a hand. "Inside."

She kicked at Konda's legs as he hauled her forward. He grunted but dragged her to the door, stopping when she threw her body weight back, resisting him. How dare they man-handle her, who the hell did Ikeda think he was?

Ikeda jerked her by the arm and Riko took a chance, shooting forward and adding to the momentum, elbowing him as she passed. He gave a shout and blood glistened, spotting the pristine surface of the Lexus. There. How'd you like that?

She spun but Konda was there. He jammed her into the car and slammed the door.

Riko scrambled across the seat. A deep 'click' bounced off the leather-bound interior. Konda hopped into the driver's seat and twisted his body to speak through a glass division. "You should do as he says. He's in a bad mood."

"Yeah?" She kicked the back of his seat. "Fuck you. Fuck you both, what the hell are you doing?"

Another click and the opposite door opened. She dived across the leather but Ikeda stood smiling, handgun levelled at her eye. Riko froze, sucking in a breath. Holy shit. She backed up, allowing him inside. Guns went far beyond intimidation.

"Drive, Konda."

"Yes, Shachō."

"Riko-san, understand that while I must and will stop you, I am not without regret." He leant closer. "But you cannot know."

He was a madman. God, what had she let him do? Allowing them to force her into the car...at least on the street she could have called out. But here? Speeding along the backstreets, to who knew where, with a gun fixed on her face and a warning from the man's own driver? Her stomach lurched.

He was still talking. "You do not know agony. How close we were, what true separation does to a soul. But how could you?" He gave a smile that was almost gentle. "You're hardly at fault, you cannot understand. Unless of course, you have loved deeply? If so, you may soon understand the barest beginning of what I have faced." His eyes flashed now. "Tell me, then, have you?"

"Loved? Yes." Her pulse raced. Just keep him talking.

"Then maybe you will not be unsympathetic."

"I don't know, maybe. Where are we going?"

He frowned. "To a quiet place."

"Why are you doing this?"

Nothing.

She waited but he only stared back at her. What was happening? He was insane. Something had changed, something was wrong and it wasn't just his eyes. He was even speaking strangely. Different to before. After a few more moments of silence and only her breathing audible, she looked away with a swallow. She had to get out. She was in trouble. She had to get away.

An old textile factory appeared ahead, its wooden boards

and dark windows mute in the darkening street. Wheels crunched on gravel in the empty car park as the Lexus stopped. Konda offered nothing from beyond the glass.

"And here we are," Ikeda said. "Once upon a time this was owned by the Ikeda family. A quiet place indeed."

The gun wove in the air between them. Her heart was thumping and her entire chest felt exposed, as if a sharp line were being traced through her skin with every movement of the gun.

"What do you want?" she asked.

"Assurance, cooperation, compliance."

She made a fist to put a stop to the trembling. "Why are you doing this to me, Ikeda?"

"Ikeda isn't doing this at all. I am."

"What?"

He shouted up to the front. "Konda."

A click.

Ikeda waved her toward the door. She took the handle and paused when he spoke. "No running now."

Konda helped her out, keeping a hand on her arm. Ikeda followed, the gun's barrel still weaving, now drawing a path from her eye, mouth and then her other eye. A bloody triangle of death.

"In we go."

Riko sucked in a breath. "People will find out."

"Undoubtedly."

Riko shoved at Konda but he held her fast, pushing her toward the entrance. His face was pale. "Just answer his questions."

Ikeda produced a key and unlocked the chain on the door. It creaked, sagging against the frame as he pushed it open. He gestured with the gun that they were to go first.

The interior fed on shadow. The only light came from lingering rays of sunset pouring through the only window without a covering. Vague shapes that might have been stalls and from the glint of steel, big sewing machines, lurked beyond the square of light. Konda stopped at a command.

Ikeda was a silhouette as he stepped into the factory, floorboards groaning.

"You're just a coward, aren't you?" Riko shouted.

"Let me ask the questions." He paused. "Where is the journal?"

Riko closed her eyes. Idiot. Of course. The Ikeda family once owned the factory. Not her captor's family. *Ikeda isn't doing this* – that's what her captor said and he meant it.

Yurei.

"You're the other man, aren't you? Saburou, the man Makiko loved before she met Hiroshi."

The ghost spat, his earlier levity dead. "Never say his name."

Konda flinched but Riko straightened. "Is this what she'd want? For you to take possession of Ikeda and murder me in the ruins of a textile factory?"

"What she wants is to be reunited with me, you filthy worm. She's in limbo – you cannot comprehend that. Now speak. Where is the journal?"

She sneered. "You're barely mentioned in it."

He growled and his eyes flashed once more. Only this time the light remained. It oozed from his shape in wisps. His voice thundered. "Speak."

"No."

The wisps twirled. "I will find it with or without you."

She said nothing.

The ghost pointed to his driver. "Retrieve the tarp from the boot, Konda."

His mouth trembled. "Tarp, sir?"

"Yes, the damn tarp. For her body."

Konda hesitated. "You said we were just going to spook her."

"We are. Now get the tarp."

"But I...I don't want to kill anyone."

A sigh. Metal caught the light and something cracked the air, a flash illumining a twisted face. Konda's grip on her arm disappeared and his body slumped to the floorboards.

Riko dove into shadow, rolling then falling still. She held her breath.

The ghost slipped deeper into the room, eyes floating in the dark. Riko moved her hands. A weapon. A piece of wood, an old sewing machine, anything would do. Nothing but dust. She drove a hand into her pocket then smothered a groan. The omamori was broken; she was a fool. And what good would it do against bullets?

"Tell me where the journal is and I will spare you."

He was lying, but which lie mattered? Did he truly need the journal, and his earlier claim a bluff? The eyes spun in a slow circle. Could he sense her? Whatever powers the ghost had must have been muted by a human body, else, why couldn't he find her?

"You must tell me." A hiss. "He's too close to her."

She could run for the door, steal the car. The ghost would have a clear shot as she crossed the threshold. If she answered, it would know where she stood, if not exactly, close enough.

But if the ghost truly needed the journal...

She rose from her crouch. "Prove it."

Riko stepped aside the moment after she spoke. The eyes spun but the gun remained silent.

"What?"

"That you'll spare me if I tell you." She moved again, back to her first position.

"I, Saburou Chiba, swear that I will spare your life if you show me the journal."

"Not good enough. Vacate his body. Follow me."

The eyes flickered.

"Or I run for the car and you kill me and you never find the journal. Hiroshi wins."

A screech rattled windows. Riko slapped hands over her ears and crouched. The eyes flared, the wisps of light elongating, rushing out and up into the roof and merging where it hovered, before streaking through the door and into the dark car park. Riko heaved a sigh, shuddering as she sat back a moment.

Ikeda gave a shout. The gun clattered to the ground. He stumbled into the last trace of light, a square from the doorway.

Riko took a parallel course into the light. "Ikeda-sama."

He spun, his eyes wide and head jerking side to side. "You? What is happening? Where am I?"

Riko looked away. "Ikeda Textile. You brought me here to kill me."

He reeled back. "Never!"

"You brought a gun and everything. Konda tried to stop you, but you shot him. It was like you were possessed."

"But I...Konda?" He shook his head. "No. Nothing is clear...this is preposterous."

She pointed. "That's his body, and there's your gun."

Ikeda's knees hit the floorboards. "My forefathers."

"And now I'm going to take your Lexus."

He twisted his torso. "Stop."

"I don't think so. You're not going to commit two murders."

"I never committed the first."

"I'm taking your car." She raised her phone. "Either that or I press 'send' on this text. Everyone in my address book will see what you did."

The bluff worked.

"I did nothing." He wrung his hands. "I did not bring you here and I did not shoot Konda."

She edged toward the door. "Smell your hands. You fired that gun. Goodbye, Ikeda-san."

He raised shaking hands to his face. A cry escaped, but she was already outside, sprinting for the car. Wrenching the door open, she dived into the driver's seat and thumped the steering wheel. God, what was happening?

A tiny Totoro figurine dangled on Konda's key chain.

Poor man.

She fired the engine, flicked the headlights on and sped from the car park. In the mirror the entry to the factory remained dark. No figure came to watch her, no ghost trailed her.

Chapter 13

Riko parked the Lexus a couple of blocks from the apartment building and walked the last bit, the muggy darkness a cloak. She kept her phone out, its glow a small comfort. Was Saburou following her? She had a small club she'd found in the car's glove box looped through her jeans, but it wouldn't do anything to a ghost.

Still, it was better than nothing.

She passed a young couple, the girl giggling behind her hand, and then turned a corner, blinking at car lights. When she could see again, Riko's heart gave a flip, a tiny acrobat in her chest.

Home.

She jogged to her Toyota. If she was quick enough, she could hide the journal from both Saburou and Kiyomi. Just so long as − locked. Riko glanced up at the house. Lights were still on. It was probably after dinner, but someone was home. What day was it?

Without her keys, she had to knock.

Kiyomi answered. She folded her arms. "When I saw

your car just sitting there unlocked, keys inside, I nearly panicked." She raised the journal. "But then I saw this. You lied."

The dam burst and every lie washed over her, oily, greasy water. She slumped. "Kiyomi, I –"

"Just come inside. You can tell it to the detective."

She stopped, whatever she was going to say vanished.

"Riko."

She removed her shoes and crossed the threshold with heavy tread. How the hell was she going to keep everything straight?

Daisuke sat across from a man in a suit. They smiled as they conversed, in the polite way that only strangers managed. The same smile she'd worn for Dad at home, leaving for the airport.

Both men rose when she entered.

"Riko Nakamura?"

"Yes."

"It's wonderful to see you unharmed." The detective appraised her and she fought off a blush. What the hell was he doing, looking her over like that? Good looking or not, pal, take it easy. "I'm Detective Watanabe. Your friends here were very persuasive. They care about you a lot; I understand you've been missing before tonight?"

"I have. I was lucky not to freeze to death." They sat, Daisuke giving her a smile. Kiyomi still held the journal, her face set as Riko explained what happened, running with her standard story. No memory. Blackouts. Her friends were wonderful for looking out for her.

The Detective opened a notepad. "I see. So, can you tell me where have you been tonight?"

"Someone..." she glanced at Kiyomi..."abducted me in front of the house."

Eyebrows climbed. "Can anyone confirm this?"

"A neighbour maybe. It was sunset."

"And did you recognise this person or persons?"

Now what, Riko? He'd have her deported. Do it. She'd never see Japan again. Just tell them. "Katashi Ikeda."

He blinked. "You are sure it was Ikeda-san?"

"Yes. He forced me into his car and drove me to an abandoned factory just out of town...but I escaped."

"How?"

"With help from his driver."

"And his name?"

"Konda. That's all I know."

"And?"

"Well, Ikeda-san hates me because he thinks I made advances toward his son. I think he was trying to scare me, but he accidently shot Konda."

Watanabe stiffened. "He murdered him?"

"It was an accident I think. When I left, he was still there. I stole his car." She couldn't look at Kiyomi or Daisuke. She stuck with Watanabe's eyes. They were narrowed.

"This is a serious allegation. If I call this in, I fully expect to find a body."

"You will."

"And there will be consequences for failing to report this immediately."

"I was afraid. I drove straight here."

He shook his head, then gave her a stern look. "If this is a lie..." He pulled a phone and dialled, launching into an explanation as soon as he received an answer. "Yes, Sergeant, get a car over to Ikeda Textile." He strode from the room.

Riko took a long drink of water.

"Is that true?" Daisuke asked. His eyes were wide.

She nodded, rubbing her eyes. If only she could get into bed already. After a good soak in the bath, just sneak beneath the covers and sleep.

The journal slapped down on the coffee table. Kiyomi stood and left without a word.

*

After dumping the journal in its usual place – she groaned, it had a 'usual place' – Riko showered. She filled the tub but didn't stay long, calling to let Kiyomi know the water was free. Her friend didn't answer and so Riko checked her bed then crawled beneath the covers. The detective hadn't called back and Daisuke left; mumbling his goodbye.

She'd already pulled a shisa from her closet. Her mother sent it along with her that first plane ride, and she'd left it in a cupboard. The little lion-like dog was cute enough, she called him Ozzy, but she didn't go for the warding off evil spirits aspect back then.

How things change.

She put the red figurine on the dresser, facing her bed, his open mouth a frozen roar. Get lost, evil spirits. Would the shisa keep Saburou away? Maybe another omamori would have been good. If it saved her from a death-spirit, surely a yurei was not stronger? Ozzy would have to do.

"I hope this works, Mum."

She clicked the lamp off, her head sinking into the pillow. Dark and warm. She exhaled, stretching her toes. Would sleep even come? Doors were locked. Ozzy was out and Kiyomi home.

She regulated her breathing until her limbs grew heavy.

Her dream was awash with pink mist.

Hiroshi stepped from the mist. He held a hand fan, which he reached out to slap her with. She swatted at him with a white paw – she was the actual Hello Kitty – but he was too fast, no matter how many times she swung her paws, he always ducked and wove, slapping her face.

He giggled as he danced, the slaps getting harder. Something pressed on her chest, slowing her.

"That's enough," she hissed as she lunged for him, sinking her claws into his neck.

Riko woke to Kiyomi sitting astride her chest in the grey dark of dawn. "Awake at last?"

"Huh? Kiyomi?"

Kiyomi slapped her cheek. "I'm waking you."

Riko struggled but her wrists were pinned, Kiyomi's knees digging in. "Get off me."

"Not until you tell me where it is."

Wisps of white light leaked from her eyes. On the dresser, beyond Kiyomi's possessed form, Ozzy faced the wall.

She drove her knee into Kiyomi's back but her friend didn't even blink. Riko hesitated. No, this was just hurting Kiyomi's body. Saburou himself was untouchable.

"Given up already?" He grinned with Kiyomi's face. "If you really want to hurt your friend, try something more fitting, like this." He leapt from the bed and slammed her head into the dresser, collapsing.

Riko screamed, shooting upright to a half-sitting position when he woozed back up. Blood streamed down her face from a split in her scalp. "How about another one?" He produced Kiyomi's pink nail file. "Or maybe if I jam this into her eye?"

"No! I'll tell you. Just leave her alone."

Kiyomi's eyes had rolled back beneath the glow. Her head was loose on her neck for a moment, then it straightened and her body moved with purpose, coming around to stand by the bed. "That's better. I'd hate to waste this one after your trickery in the factory." He put a hand on her own and squeezed. "It took time to find a way into her, Riko. Longer than Ikeda. She was strong too, but there was a chink. Her fury. She is awfully angry with you." Again, the smile that wasn't Kiyomi's.

Riko gritted her teeth. "And you'll leave her too, when I show you the journal?"

A short nod. "I want only the journal."

She slipped from the bed, pulling her loose shirt down as far over her bare legs as it would reach. The burning eyes traced her every move. Riko slid the wardrobe open and moved the basket, pulling the journal free.

He snatched it from her grasp, flicking through the pages. "Finally." A frown grew, the deeper he went into the book. He glared up at her. "Some of the pages are stuck together."

"It was lying beneath the forest floor." Riko stepped forward. "Now you can leave her."

The journal snapped shut. "No."

"I'll stop you."

"How?" He strode to the door.

Riko leapt after him, pulling Kiyomi's shoulders back. Saburou spun, dropping the journal to catch her hands. He flung her onto the bed with barely a flick of his wrists. "I think I'll take her with me." Then he retrieved the journal and ran for the door. Riko tossed the blankets aside, leapt into her crumpled jeans and stumbled outside.

Saburou strode toward Kiyomi's car.

Riko dashed back inside and grabbed her shoes and bag, then stopped. Kiyomi would have found her keys yesterday. She ran to the kitchen. There. Snatching them from the bench, she sprinted after the ghost, spilling onto the front lawn in time to see Saburou back into her car, smashing in the rear passenger door before roaring onto the quiet road.

"Bastard." Riko ran around her car and jumped in, screeching after her hostage friend.

The road was near to empty this early, Kiyomi's taillights easy to follow. The ghost sped along the freeway, slipping round the few other vehicles on the road. Before he turned, Riko knew which path he would take.

Lake Saiko.

Several times he tried to lose her, by slamming the brakes on and faking turns, but she kept her distance and matched his pace. Light grew in the sky, and by the time she closed in it was full light. He'd pulled up in the car park, running for the hiking trail. Riko squeezed her shoes on and charged after him.

Did he know how to find Hiroshi's tree? Of course he would.

Kiyomi ran on. Riko breathed hard, pumping her arms. The trees closed in around them. She leapt over a fallen branch, slipping as she landed, but keeping her feet somehow. Saburou was putting more distance between them. At every turn, up every slope, he charged ahead, driving Kiyomi's body with his unnatural strength. With his jealousy.

She was too slow. Before each turn, Saburou would slip from sight. By the time she reached the familiar clearing, her legs buckled. She fell to her hands and knees, swearing between gasps.

He wasn't even visible anymore.

Shouting voices forced their way into her ears. She looked up. A group of school kids, girls with high socks and boys with their ties loosened, stood around her. Was she all right? Did she want water? She could use his National Soccer Team bottle if she wanted. A teacher knelt beside her.

"Ma'am, are you feeling okay?" He surveyed her through his glasses.

"Yes, I just need to rest."

He handed her a water bottle. "Here."

She gulped it down and sat back a moment. "I'm sorry to cause a scene. I'm just out of shape."

The girls giggled and the teacher shooed them away. "Are you racing the other woman or something?"

"Is she here?"

"No. She went off onto one of the trails. She was running quite fast."

"She's pretty strong." Riko said, taking another drink. "Thank you."

He nodded. "I can't help but notice you don't have any gear. Have you hiked here before?"

Her bag was back in the car. She stood. "Yeah, a few times."

"All right." He said the words slowly. "Well, good luck with your friend."

"Thanks." Riko crossed the picnic area, letting the students' chatter wash over her. She'd barely taken half a dozen steps when she stopped.

Hiroshi stood by the water's edge.

Chapter 14

White hair caught in the breeze and his shoulders were slumped beneath a green coat. He held no rake and she saw, moving around to stand beside him, that his eyes were misted. He stared across the lake. Did he even notice he was no longer alone?

"Hiroshi?"

He turned at her voice and frowned. "You again?" He shook his head. "Don't know why you're following me, young lady. If you're a reporter, well, you'd better stop, and no more lies."

"No. I tried to tell you before. I found Makiko's journal."

His face went slack.

"It was in the woods nearby. Buried."

"Makiko?"

"Yes. She talks about your life together."

He took her shoulders. "You have it here?"

"No. It was stolen –"

"What?"

Riko broke his grip. "I tried to give it to you at your house but you didn't let me. You just lost control."

Hiroshi opened his mouth to retort but turned back to the water. "I am sorry about that." After a moment, he continued, voice quiet. "But I'm finished now anyway."

She moved closer. "Hiroshi, we can get it back. I know where it is."

"How?"

"I don't know if you'll believe me."

"Young lady, whoever you are, you'd be surprised what I believe. If you're serious, I want to know."

"My name is Riko."

"Very well, Riko. Tell me."

She took a breath. "All right. A ghost has it. He took control of my friend Kiyomi and now he's run off into the forest. I was trying to catch him. But he's superhuman or something."

"Just now?"

"I think he's heading for your oak."

Recognition flashed in his eyes. "Follow me." Hiroshi strode off toward the trees, coat flapping. Riko hurried after him, ducking into the chill beneath the twisted branches. Hiroshi took them along a path she'd never used before. Where was Saburou? Behind each tree, beyond every weird hump in the ground, each black opening, was he waiting? Ready to leap out and throttle them? Club her to death with a log?

Sunlight flickered down to speckle the loam. Her feet stirred earthy scents. Without hiking shoes it was hard work, but she managed to keep up with Hiroshi. And thankfully, there was probably no chance of meeting the death-spirit again, not in the morning, in the light of day. "What did you mean, before, about being finished?"

He stopped. "I've been searching for her journal for years. I think she hid it from me. In shame."

"She wrote about you with a lot of love."

Hiroshi pressed his lips together. "This ghost. It is Makiko's first husband, isn't it? Saburou?"

"Yes."

"Bastard."

"What's he going to do with the journal?"

"Keep it from me." Hiroshi looked into the trees and his voice softened. "She felt guilty but there was no betrayal, I told her so many times. He died in the war; it was years before we met. She was too hard on herself."

Riko nearly reached for his hand. Her suicide had obviously gutted him. What was left for Hiroshi now? His whole life had changed. Was there only obsession? The gathering and burning of her possessions? Didn't it hurt, to do that to things she'd once touched? "Surely she loved you more? The love of an adult, not the whimsy of a teenager?"

He glanced at her before starting off again. "Perhaps."

A small fire burned clear beneath his tree. No sign of Saburou. Damn him, what had he done with Kiyomi? Hiroshi deserved the journal and Riko needed her friend alive and well; who knew what taint the ghost would leave?

"Not here," Hiroshi said. "But he'll be close."

"Did he leave a trail?" Riko turned a slow circle. The taste of ash lay heavy on the air. Leaves fluttered to the floor.

"Not that I see, but I'm watching." He strode to the trunk and took up his rake.

Riko met his gaze. "He's using my friend's body."

Hiroshi nodded but said nothing.

Squawking broke the hush. Two birds bickered above her

then burst from the foliage in a mess of leaves and feathers. Riko sidestepped to track them, but stopped. Something large rested in the higher branches.

An odd shape. Dark, darker than the bark around it and resting...no, attached to the tree. A growth? Some massive bunch of fruit? She squinted. Saburou hiding up there in some sort of cloak? No. Something else.

Riko reached for the lowest branch.

"Don't." Hiroshi strode over to her. "It's not safe for Makiko."

"What?"

He gestured to the tree and the raked grass. "Do you know what I do here?"

"The rangers said you were burning her possessions."

"It's more than that." He chuckled. "I must sound like a crazy man."

"Maybe."

"I've been coming here for thirty years. First with Makiko and later...only to visit. Just to see the tree and sit and remember. We used to hike Saiko and once, we left the trail. I didn't care to, truly, but Makiko was curious. You know about Aokigahara."

She nodded.

"Well, we didn't find anything but this beautiful old oak." He rested a hand against the bark. "Makiko loved it and so we came back every anniversary. But once she was gone..."

Riko looked to a pile of ash. "You started burning her things?"

"That was later." He said. "Her blue headscarf first. I was going to tie it to a branch. But I had a vision of burning it beneath the tree. So I set the scarf aflame and when it was burnt, I covered what little ash was left in leaves and returned home. Makiko sent the vision, I realised later."

Riko kept her voice gentle. "You burnt a lot." In a way, Hiroshi had become a deer. A sudden movement or loud noise might break the spell, might chase his memories away. Even the frown lines in his face had eased.

"Clothes, books, jewellery, furniture. Even a television." He smiled. "That took some doing. But I burnt everything I could find, anything she'd owned. Each time I went home, I had a vision of something else she wanted me to burn."

"So she was erasing herself?"

He shook his head, and his eyes burned. "No, girl. The opposite. She was collecting herself for me. For the future."

"Collecting?"

"In this place. Everything about her." Hiroshi gripped the rake. "Everything but the journal. I searched and searched and after everything it was buried in the forest – it was this close for so long!"

"You couldn't know."

"But I should have."

"She didn't tell you?"

"For the last couple of years her messages have been cloudy. I've been guessing."

"Oh." Riko glanced around the clearing. Still no sign of Kiyomi. "How does it work?"

He smiled now. "Easy. Our tree catches the smoke. Absorbs it right into the leaves and the bark. Still believe me?"

"Ah –"

"I didn't notice with the scarf, but later I saw. And when the leaves fell that autumn, I raked them up and burnt them too. Every year I do it. I have to make sure each part of her stays in the tree until the right time."

Riko looked to the oak. It did sound crazy. But then, no crazier than a ghost with flaming eyes or a journal that stalked her or anything else that had happened. Somehow, it made sense, what Hiroshi said. But what she really wanted to know was why Makiko chose her? "The first time I saw this place, it was smoke I followed. It led me here."

"It must have been Makiko. Not all the smoke feeds in anymore. It's nearly full. Look." He moved over to point up to the large shape high in the branches. Riko felt her eyes widen. It *did* have the vague shape of a woman. Not unlike the carvings Hiroshi had made, only now curled, long hair flowing. And it *was* growing from one of the branches, like a giant piece of fruit. A human fruit.

Makiko.

Waiting to be reborn.

"But..."

"Beautiful, isn't she?"

Riko could only nod.

"It's taken years and years to get this close. If I could just burn the journal, she'd finally come back. It's the last piece, I know it. It has her heart, her soul within – her writing. Her most private thoughts. The missing piece."

"She'll be resurrected, whole?"

He nodded. "For now her spirit is trapped. Saburou must have some hold on her or she would have returned already. Or maybe it's me, tying her to the earth?" He thumped the rake on the grass. "But it's nearly over now. With the journal I can finish it."

"But how do we stop Saburou?"

"There'll be an opportunity. He wants to gloat."

"I don't want Kiyomi to get hurt."

Hiroshi's face hardened. "I'm not making promises, girl. If your friend is possessed, who knows what's been done to her? Might never be the same."

She caught his arm. "Well she's alive now."

A figure stepped into the clearing. "Yes, for now she is alive." Saburou stood with the journal in hand, wisps of light still seeping from Kiyomi's eyes.

Chapter 15

Hiroshi pointed with his rake. "Give me her journal, Saburou. You had your time."

"And you yours. I've watched you for years, old man, waiting for my chance. Doing whatever I could to disrupt this sick ritual." He paced the edge of the clearing. "But you will keep her from me no more."

Riko moved closer to Hiroshi. "She's rejected you, hasn't she, Saburou?"

"That has yet to be decided." He raised the journal. "But I have the last piece of her. I've made certain of that. It is a precious, glorious gift, to see her words."

"Give it up," Hiroshi snapped.

"You see, I cannot – after I read the journal I took a precaution. I have eaten a single page. If you wish to complete your rebirth, you will have to kill this poor young lady."

Riko gasped.

Hiroshi lowered the rake. "You what?"

He laughed. "The ultimate insurance." Saburou kept his pacing. Beyond him, the forest darkened as the sun moved behind a cloud. "Now, one of you cut that abomination down and the other can build up the fire. Time to free Makiko's spirit."

"No."

"Fine," he snapped. "Then I will impale this girl on your rake then take Riko there, or you yourself, old man, and complete the task."

Riko faced Hiroshi. "She's my friend."

"And Makiko is my wife."

Saburou crossed his arms. "Hurry." The darkness grew behind him. Riko turned. Within the clearing, the light remained as day, but beyond its borders the shadows deepened.

"What's happening?" she asked.

"The coming night?" He smiled. "I've hardly been idle while you two chatted. I invited someone to clear up any lingering sense of defiance you might have."

In the shadows a huge shape loomed in the distance. Shinigami.

Its white linen kimono barely rustled as it moved, pale face and downturned mouth solidifying as it neared. Black hair fell in straight lines and the clicking of its bone necklace filled the hush.

Riko's hand shot to her jeans pocket, to the omamori. Her pulse doubled. Still broken. She didn't have anything. Hiroshi's jaw was clenched but he stood his ground. "A god of death, that's your friend, Saburou?"

"Do as I say and I won't have to invite him in."

Hiroshi threw his rake aside and charged Saburou, hands outstretched. The ghost smiled, even as Riko stumbled after the old man. Hiroshi wrapped his arms around Kiyomi's neck and a white light blazed, so bright it stung her eyes, even as she looked away. The old man's scream was buried beneath the white, and when it cleared, he was on his hands and knees, scrambling back.

The ghost pointed to Riko. "Save three lives and build up that fire." He sneered down at Hiroshi, twisting Kiyomi's slack face. "You stay put."

Hiroshi swore, pushing himself up on trembling legs, only to fall back to the grass.

Riko stepped into the black, blinking when the forest became light. It didn't matter. She had to save everyone, which meant sacrificing Makiko. She'd lived once; Hiroshi would have to accept it.

Riko collected branches and heavier logs too. One was a fair heft. She shivered. Was it worth using as a weapon? A piece of wood to take on a powerful spirit? Knocking Kiyomi down would do nothing. She was already unconscious, Saburou would simply keep using her. There had to be something she could do.

Back within the circle of light, the ghost had climbed the tree and was sawing at the Makiko-fruit with Kiyomi's nail file – only the pink-handle and blade were now large as something from a hardware store.

The shinigami stood motionless beyond the clearing.

Riko bit her lip. How in God's name had Saburou become so strong? Was he fuelled by his obsession? Did he feed off the forest itself? Or maybe he drew strength from the shinigami – if that was even possible. Who knew? Who cared? She had to keep it away. Riko dumped the wood into a stack and shouted up to Saburou. "There. Now you can call off the shinigami."

Hiroshi groaned as sparks leapt from the pile of wood.

The sawing paused and tendrils of light stared down at her. "Let's be sure, first – shall we?"

The sawing resumed until a splitting filled the clearing. The woman-shaped fruit fell to the ground with a thud. Hiroshi cried out, crawling forward, eyes wide and staring, hands feeling about the grass in desperation. The flash of light had blinded him.

Makiko's wooden cocoon rolled toward the fire, coming to a halt at its edge. A wind whipped through the clearing, stirring the pages of the journal. It lay in the grass at the foot of the tree. Saburou must have dropped it to climb and saw. She dashed forward, ignoring the cry from above, and cast the journal into the flames.

A branch snapped. In the tree, Kiyomi's body was ensnared and Saburou screeched, eyes blazing as he struggled to free himself.

"Help me." Riko tugged Hiroshi to his feet and guided him to Makiko. Tears streamed down his face as together, they lifted Makiko and held her sleeping form over the flames. The heat seared Riko's fingers but the smoke was absorbed into the wood. "It's working."

"Steady," Hiroshi commanded. She lifted her end higher. Makiko's cocoon blushed with colour, a warm orange. It spread along the grain, as if a glittering fire lay deep inside.

From the tree the screeching continued but Riko saw only the quickening wood.

And then it stopped, fading, pulsing.

"You need the final page," Saburou hissed. He was free now, hurrying down to leer at her. He knew she couldn't push her friend into the flames.

"Move her," Hiroshi gasped out. Riko set Makiko down on the grass. The glow faded further and Hiroshi collapsed before the wooden fruit, running his wrinkled hands over the surface. "She's lost forever," he cried.

Bones clinked.

The shinigami stepped into the circle, eyes closed. Saburou was waving it on. Could the death-spirit take a spirit? Saburou was probably safe. The ghost stood behind Hiroshi, who'd reached his knees, head twisting from sound to sound.

"You must choose, Riko. Kill your friend to try completing the rebirth? Or perhaps die now, along with both Kiyomi and the old man?" He pointed at her. "Or do you actually value your life enough to help me?"

Hiroshi's mouth worked but he wasn't speaking. Riko's shoulders slumped. "How can I trust you?"

"Because once Makiko's spirit is free, I will have no need for this body. I must meet her as spirit." Saburou's expression was one of supreme confidence, standing beside the blind Hiroshi, the shinigami towering in the background, hands by its side.

Riko made a fist. "Fine. Fine! I'm sorry, Hiroshi. But Makiko has lived. I have to save my friend."

He choked out half a word, but seemed spent. He didn't move and tears streamed from his sightless eyes, his misery complete.

Wait. Was that the answer?

Saburou only held power over them if he could threaten their lives. If she took that power away from him...but could she make such a sacrifice? Could she fail to make it? Could Kiyomi afford hesitation?

Riko walked forward, keeping her eyes downcast, as if defeated. She stopped before Hiroshi. She bent down and caught his hands. She leant in to kiss his cheek. "Do you trust me?"

"What?"

"Trust me. Everything will work out." She took a breath, then drove both hands into Hiroshi's chest. He flew back with a cry, rolling into the shinigami. The moment his flailing limbs touched the pool of black hair and the robe, his voice was cut short and his body collapsed into a heap.

Riko fell back, stomach churning. He was gone.

God, had she done the right thing?

The shinigami's hands rose, dirt falling between its fingers, and it slowly arranged Hiroshi's body on the grass. It moved with a stately grace, straightening first his legs and then his arms. Tiny puffs of dust rose whenever its hands paused, and the animal and human skulls knocked together in a sombre music.

Saburou gaped at the scene, disbelief pouring from him in waves.

She had to keep moving. Finish it, Riko. She clenched her teeth but kept her own movement glacial. A twist of the ankle, a turn of the knee, a soft step, bend down, reach out... her hands gripped Makiko's wooden form. The surface was cool and dark, it rocked gently beneath the weight of her palm. It was so much lighter; had Makiko started to leave already? She braced herself and spun, heaving it onto the flames.

The shell disappeared in a whoosh of orange.

Saburou whirled. Tendrils slithered from Kiyomi's eyes, ears, mouth and nose now. "What have you done?"

"I've reunited them," she shouted. It was the only way to stop Saburou. It had to be. Otherwise she'd made a hideous mistake.

"No! She is mine, I loved her first."

"You've failed, Saburou – now give Kiyomi back. There's nothing here for you now, the journal, the sacrifice, none of it means anything now. Makiko and Hiroshi are together, give her up."

The eyes flickered. "This is your price to pay now, usurper."

Riko stood her ground. "You started this."

Kiyomi jerked forward, leaping over the flame and crashing into Riko. Fingernails dug into her throat and she beat at her friend's arms, but Saburou did not let go.

His tendrils turned dark.

Bright spots burst across Riko's vision. She rasped for air, chest constricting. The oak tree faded, only Kiyomi's face, twisted in rage, remained beyond the spots. Riko kept beating on her attacker's arms, but they had turned to stone for all the good it did.

She'd join Hiroshi and Makiko soon.

Did it matter?

Wait, no. Where did that thought come from?

And yet, she wouldn't have to worry about Dad anymore; his disappointment, his illnesses. Not Mum's worry either. Explaining all the lies away, winning back Kiyomi's trust. Dealing with Yuuki's father; the police; her job. Being deported.

Life lay poised on a knifepoint.

Wings swept down, surrounding her in a gentle cage of feathers, black and white everywhere. Her breathing eased. A long beak and liquid eyes hovered before her, and when the head turned to snap at something Riko couldn't see, a red stripe was revealed. It ran down the crane's head and along its back.

The bird turned its gaze back to her and the animal face wavered until a woman's face replaced it. Of an age with Riko's mother, her smile was gentle and her dark eyes crinkled at the corners.

"Be at ease."

Makiko.

Chapter 16

Snow crunched underfoot when Makiko helped her up.

The pressure of fingers at Riko's throat was gone, the memory of Kiyomi's weight on her chest vague. Even her limbs were light and she shivered – not from the cold, but a long sigh of relief.

Safe.

She stood in the same clearing, only now the oak was black with winter-ice, a network of bare branches sitting against a white sky that clung to blushes of pink. Barren, and yet beautiful, too. Was this some sort of spirit-world? Heaven in winter? Thunder boomed, faint, but no storm clouds lurked on the horizon.

It didn't seem like she was dead, but what would she know?

Makiko waited nearby, hands near-to-lost in the sleeves of her black kimono. Riko opened her mouth to thank the woman, to ask about Saburou, about where they were, was she even alive – but she couldn't make a sound.

Makiko was unfinished.

Parts of the snowy landscape were visible through her

robe, even a large half-circle in her neck and flecks in her hair.

Her smile deepened. "Riko, you must be concerned and confused. But know you are alive and all is well. Will you help me at the tree?"

"Of course, thank you." She joined the older woman at the trunk, which glistened in the winter air, and knelt in the snow. There was no cold and when she reached out to copy Makiko, who brushed away the snow, her fingers remained warm and dry.

"What are we…" she trailed off. Someone was buried beneath the snow. Clothing…shoulders…a face. She flinched back.

Thunder cracked again.

"It's only Hiroshi," Makiko said. She glanced at the sky with a slight frown before brushing the last of the snow from his cheeks. Riko shuddered. This wasn't what she'd imagined when she played her last, desperate ploy. In death all the anger was gone from his face, the lines softened – and she'd killed him.

"I'm sorry, I didn't think…"

"Do not be sad."

She spun to face Makiko. "Honestly, I couldn't think of anything else. I thought it was the only way. Saburou was supposed to give up once he had nothing to hold over us, Makiko, I only wanted –"

Makiko put a hand on her own. "Don't worry about that now. Let's lift him up."

"All right." Riko took a shoulder and helped raise him, snow fluttering to the ground soundlessly. Makiko leant in and kissed his blue lips and stepped back, one hand still holding him. Riko kept hold at a nod from Makiko, then blinked when Hiroshi's eyes snapped open.

He cried out but when he saw Makiko he quietened. Hiroshi's eyes filled as he reached out to brush her cheek with his fingers.

"Makiko," he breathed.

Riko moved away. They deserved a moment alone – as alone as Riko dared anyway, wandering off in the white... place...was probably a bad idea. She stared across the snow to the pale sky. Mt Fuji should have been visible, not to mention the forest itself. Only there was naught but a distant glow hovering where sky met land, as if a giant paint set had fallen and orange and pink had clashed.

"Riko."

Hiroshi and Makiko stood before her. "Are you all right?" she asked.

He nodded. "Better. Thank you."

"You're not angry that I...killed you?"

He laughed. "Wasn't what I planned but I'm happy. You thought on your feet." He faced his wife and now regret replaced his laughter. "I wanted to bring you home. We could have finished the garden and the –"

She placed a finger against his lips. "But we are together now."

"You're right."

"And perhaps for the better," she said. "I was...in a hell and you drew me forth, even as you trapped me in that tree, beloved."

"I trapped you?" His face was almost comical in its distress. "But I was close, only the journal remained and..." he trailed off when Makiko laughed at him, a hand covering her mouth.

"Just be pleased. It is my turn to protect you."

He smiled.

Thunder roared overhead, rocking the oak. Riko looked to the sky. "Are we safe here? And what about Saburou and Kiyomi?"

"Ah." Makiko's own smile fell. "I have driven him from your friend, but he makes trouble yet."

"That's him, making the thunder?"

"Yes."

Hiroshi shook his head. "Fool. He's failed."

"But he cannot accept it," Makiko said.

"Can't you stop him?" Riko asked.

"Perhaps. I am slow to recover my strength. Being trapped inside our tree for so long, I haven't been able to change much at all in the living-world."

"But you sent me messages didn't you? Like the smoke? You can still do things."

"I did. Although often as I tried, Saburou interfered. He has never stopped watching me. But the ancestors must have granted me luck to lead you to the journal. Toward the end, poor Hiroshi could never hear me." She glanced at him. "You have quite the one-track mind, sometimes."

"You used to say I was focused."

She smiled again but a sigh followed. "Well, no matter. Once you neared the end of your task, Saburou began to scatter every message I tried to send you anyway. As his jealousy and fear grew so did his strength – though I feel it ebbing now."

"But what about Kiyomi?" Riko asked.

"She is alive but we should be sure of Saburou. Your

friend is vulnerable to him still." Makiko held out a hand. "Come, we will put an end to his madness together."

Riko hesitated. "I can't do anything, I'm just –"

"Nonsense. Lend me your strength."

Their hands met and the tree began to recede. Makiko blew a kiss over her shoulder to the waiting Hiroshi, whose expression was uncertain, and then the clearing, the snow, the breath-of-fire sky, all of it was gone and they were flying.

She rushed through air, though her body still lay on the grass in the world of the living. Everything was soft. The wind gentle, a hint of the ocean on it and beneath, the entire forest spread in a green sea. Lake Saiko flashed blue. The crane had returned. Its wings tilted and they dipped, gliding down, each movement smooth.

"Makiko?"

She gave no answer, save for a tensing of muscles and a dip in their flight. Makiko swooped low and Riko's stomach flipped. The treetops rushed up and then another plunge as the crane skimmed the surface of the lake. Riko reached down and bounced fingertips along the water.

Something shimmered ahead.

A black shape flew across the lake, skipping and dodging. Saburou. The crane tracked its movements, gaining ground steadily until the spirit splashed beneath the surface. The crane speared the water and Riko took a deep breath as darkness surrounded them.

Only she needed no air.

And Makiko was no longer a crane. Instead, Riko clung to a giant goldfish of shimmering white. It cleaved black water, chasing Saburou – though where he was in the depths of the lake was impossible to tell. Makiko twisted in the water, changing direction, then arching down and thrusting up toward a blue glow. It was like a soundless rollercoaster. The white fish burst from the water and splashed onto a cave floor.

In the corner a shadow lurked, blue light bouncing from its edges.

A young man in an army uniform resolved from the shade. He inched forward, smooth hands outstretched. Riko flinched when he reached the light. His face was twisted, deep lines carved into greying skin, his teeth ground down to nubs and eyes pig-like, buried in dark sockets.

"Makiko, please. Forgive all I have done. I wanted only to be reunited with you. As we promised each other." He hesitated. "Please, why can't I see you?"

A fox sat beside Riko, licking its paws. It, too, was white with red tufts around its paws and striped down its head and back. Jaws snapped. "No, Saburou. Look at yourself. At what you've become."

"Please. I never forgot." His voice rose to a whine. "Please, what of our time together, does it mean nothing?"

Makiko growled. "You tainted those memories with your childish behaviour."

He fell to his knees. "But for decades I waited for you. Watched you, tried to protect you from Hiroshi – that's what you wanted, wasn't it? That's why you took your life, to be reunited with me?"

"No!" The Fox's fur turned black and it stood first on hind legs then two feet, as it morphed into Makiko's human form. "My shame was my own, Saburou. And in your madness, you betrayed me. Our love."

"Beloved."

"No longer. And for what you have done, I am cursing you, Saburou." She gestured for Riko to come closer then locked her hand in her own grip. "For it is here you shall stay, alone with naught but the lap of water on stone, for eternity. Never to see, to hear or speak with me or another again."

Riko cried out, pitching forward. Something sharp cut into the very essence of her, white hot. It sapped her strength, sending it coursing down her arm, through her hand and into Makiko, leaving behind aching emptiness.

"Stand your ground, young lady," Makiko whispered, holding tight. "Remember what he did to you, to your friend. To me."

Riko clenched her teeth, dragging herself upright. "I will."

She fed all her rage, hurt and fear into the woman holding her. It followed her strength, passing from skin to skin before it shot forth from Makiko's free hand, making a crystalline wall that shimmered once then disappeared.

Saburou shot to his feet with a screech but he could step no closer. He beat against the unseen wall with his ragged hands and even his head. With each strike his face distorted yet further. It blackened and steamed and Riko flinched when he gurgled.

Finally he fell back with a long groan, shrinking into the corner.

Makiko released her hand. "There. Now your friend is safe. And thank you, Riko, for answering my call. Without you there would only be pain for us."

Riko heaved a breath. "You're welcome."

Makiko smiled as her face elongated, becoming fox-like, and she beckoned with one paw as the lithe creature leapt into the water.

How, she didn't know, but Riko followed.
Heading home.

Chapter 17

A deep quiet filled the sunny clearing.

Not a single bird sang, no breeze moved even a blade of grass. The oak tree was still. The forest beyond was no longer dark, but a hazy green and yellow light cloaked it – as if in a fairy tale.

Maybe not so unlikely.

Riko sat up. The fire was no more than a pile of ash and char and Hiroshi's body no-where to be seen. The shinigami was gone too. All that remained were tiny piles of dirt by the edge of the clearing.

A cool breath of air stirred the hairs on her arm.

"Oh."

Kiyomi lay nearby, face bruised, rivulets of dried blood running from forehead to cheek. Her leg lay twisted and blood from cuts and scrapes on her arms and body stained her clothes. Her lips were cracked and dry. Blessedly, her chest rose and fell in a thin rhythm.

Riko took Kiyomi's hand. A frown crossed her brow but she did not wake. Carrying her friend from the forest would be impossible, Riko herself was still weak after helping

Makiko. Night would fall soon enough and then who knew what would happen?

Trees parted and Akio the ranger appeared, a shocked expression on his face. He was almost like a cartoon, scratching his head. He blinked when he saw them.

Akio dashed over. "Are you all right? What happened?"

"Akio, thank god you're here."

"Excuse me?" Recognition dawned. "Again? What happened to your friend?"

"She fell from the oak."

"Did she?" He checked her pulse, then stood, clicking on a radio. "Tetsu, I'll be late back, just helping someone out of the forest."

Tetsu's voice crackled back. "Idiots. All right."

"Why was she climbing Hiroshi's tree?" Akio removed a piece of white cloth and bottled water from his pack, dabbing at some of the blood on Kiyomi's face.

"I think she was on something," Riko said. How easy the lies came, even now. No more of that when Kiyomi was better. But Saburou was trapped, so she wouldn't need to lie anyway. And wouldn't Kiyomi believe her now? "How did you find us?"

Akio paused. "I was following a white fox...or so I thought." He smiled. "Doesn't matter now."

Thank you, Makiko. Riko nodded, letting him finish cleaning up Kiyomi. "All right. Let's get your friend out of here." He gestured. "Grab her legs, will you? Just be careful."

She lifted and together, with some difficulty, carried Kiyomi out of the forest and into the picnic area. There Akio called for emergency services but it still took a couple of hours for a group of paramedics to emerge from the trees and begin setting up a stretcher.

Akio spoke with one of the men. Riko studied the ground at her feet. Ants made tiny pilgrimages across the leaves and twigs.

"Come along." One of the servicemen touched her shoulder.

She stood, glancing at Akio. "Thank you."

He smiled. "Forgive me, but I hope you don't visit Saiko for a while. For your own health, that is."

Riko grinned. "No promises."

But she wouldn't. The last few days and everything that went with them needed time to fade into memory. For now, they were too real. Too bright in her mind. The feel of Hiroshi's chest beneath her palms, the chill calm of the death-spirit, the wonder of Makiko's spirit flying her into the lake.

Saburou's blackened face.

The long walk back to the car park was done in a blink, though her legs were lead weights as she slumped into the car seat.

"Do you want one of us to drive?" It was the same paramedic.

She shook her head. "I'll be fine, thank you."

"All right. We're taking her to Fuji-Yoshida City Hospital, okay?"

She turned the key and followed the ambulance along the highway, into the city and to the hospital, followed the stretcher on its wheels to the waiting room and stood on her tiptoes as Kiyomi was wheeled into an emergency room.

A nurse took her to a waiting room. "You'll have to wait here."

Riko nodded as she slumped into a chair, folded her legs up and leaned her head back.

Closed her eyes.

Someone touched her shoulder. Riko groaned as she straightened. The hospital waiting room – winningly white – was broken by a nurse in green surgical gear. How long had she slept? Riko swallowed, throat dry. "Yes?"

"Your friend is awake. Would you like to speak with her?"

"Yes. Is she all right?"

"She's recovering well enough but there's a lot of hard work ahead."

Riko followed the woman down quiet corridors, stalked by the beeping and the laser blue of medical machines. Rushing in with Kiyomi earlier, old fears had taken a backseat to new ones. What if Kiyomi died? What if she was horribly changed somehow and the doctors couldn't fix her?

But the old fears returned now, sneaking through the sterile smell of the place and hitting her hard. Her shoulders twitched with every beep.

Dad, tubes and bandages. Drips looming; vampiric. Or so it seemed to her wide, five-year-old eyes. Even the rasp of his voice, as he called for a nurse, the way Mum shook as she tried to lift him back onto the bed and the whole time the scream of emergency alarms from somewhere else in the hospital, until she crept forward, reached out to help, only to flinch when her small hands encountered clammy skin.

The way his eyes didn't see her, through the pain.

And when Mum finally got him back into bed he laid back with eyes screwed shut and jammed a thumb into the button of what looked like a small TV remote – a light flashing above the bed with every press.

"In here." The nurse said. "Just not long, all right? She needs rest."

Riko blinked. Kiyomi. "I understand."

The room was bare but for bed and television mounted on the ceiling. A powder blue curtain ringed the bed, creating a cocoon of screen-glow. Kiyomi would be inside, maybe dozing, maybe weak from the medication. Maybe hurt forever. Just like Dad.

Riko hesitated.

Bullshit, go in there. She needs a friend, not a coward.

She took a few steps and by the time she drew the curtain back her hand was steady. Kiyomi lay propped up by pillows, connected to a drip. Her face was clean, her arm bandaged and her leg covered in a cast. Cuts on her face and hands had been cleaned and dressed too, and her hair fanned the pillow. Cleaned. Everything, cleaned.

Except Riko's conscience.

"Kiyomi?"

Her eyes fluttered open. She smiled. "Riko."

Riko smiled back as she eased herself into a chair and took Kiyomi's hand. "Are you in a lot of pain?"

"Not really. The drugs must be good."

A weak laugh.

Kiyomi patted her hand. "Come on, it's all right. I know, Riko."

"Huh?"

"I saw enough through Saburou's eyes. I thought what he thought." She shuddered, squeezing Riko's hand. "He kind of...pushed me...off to the side. But I understood more than enough."

"Oh."

"I wish you'd been able to tell me the truth."

"Me too."

She frowned and it didn't seem to be from discomfort. "I could have been there for you."

Tears built. "I know this doesn't make it right, but, do you think you would have believed the whole story, if I tried to tell you?"

Kiyomi sighed. "I guess not. But it still hurt."

"I know. I'm sorry."

Kiyomi sighed. "Well, are you okay?"

"I suppose I am now." She paused. "And we're okay?"

"We are."

"I'm so sorry I lied. I hated it."

She gave a small smile. "I probably would have kept it secret too. Just promise me we won't keep anything from each other again, all right?"

"Deal." She smiled back. "So what now?"

"Now I do what it takes to get out of here – I'll hardly see you if I stay too long. I know how much you love hospitals."

"I'll visit," Riko said, keeping her voice firm. "I mean it."

"Good."

"Did they tell you anything?"

"Not much. Or maybe I just don't remember what they said." She scratched at her wrist, near the IV. "The break is serious so I'll have physio for recovery and they're monitoring the knock to the head...I'm not sure."

"It's fine. You should rest," Riko said, standing.

Kiyomi pointed with a grin. "No, you should get some rest – proper rest. You've got fabric creases on your cheek. Go home, I'm fine. Mum and Dad will be here later."

Riko put a hand to her cheek. Grooves. "Good idea."

Kiyomi's own eyelids were getting heavy. Riko stroked her friend's hair back from her face and slipped from the room. She drove home with the window down, cold air blasting her face. Even so, she blinked half a dozen streets into oblivion, pulling up before her building with a jolt, stopping inches from the car in front.

Detective Watanabe stepped from the vehicle.

Chapter 18

"Shall we talk inside?"

Riko nodded, leading the way to the kitchen. Was Watanabe here to arrest her? He didn't seem like he was about to break out the handcuffs – he wasn't even in uniform, just a shirt and slacks.

"Tea, Detective?"

"Please."

She filled the kettle and took out two mugs. The soft clunk when they hit the benchtop was loud. Maybe he was just following up on Ikeda. "Sugar?"

"Three please."

She complied, and the other cup she made strong enough to animate a statue. "Wow, that's very sweet."

"What can I say? My dentist is a magnificent man."

She sat across from him, blowing on her coffee. "Did you find Konda and Ikeda?"

"Yes."

"And?"

"It appears that Ikeda-san did fire the gun that killed

Konda."

"He admitted as much?"

"The evidence was clear."

Riko took a long sip. Her secret remained secret for now. "And are there charges against me?"

"That I will reconsider, if you can tell me more about why you thought he abducted you. It seems a rash act for a man such as Ikeda-san."

"I thought it rash myself."

Did he fight off a smile? "Go on."

"Well, he already had me. He could have found a way to cancel my visa easily enough. And he's friends with my ex-sponsor."

"Yes, so why bother taking you?" He took a drink. "And yet he did. Do you think, perhaps, that he was attracted to you?"

She frowned. "That doesn't make sense."

"Perhaps." He stared at her, then looked away and cleared his throat. He stood. "Well, I should be leaving."

That was all? Riko joined him. What if there was a trial? It wouldn't look good for someone on a visa to be involved in a murder. "Will I have to testify or go to court?"

"No."

"Won't there be a trial?"

"I found Ikeda-san's body in his home. He had committed suicide."

"Oh." Riko put her cup down. How would Yuuki be handling his father's death? Poor kid. But it might be good news too. "And my working visa?"

"I cannot make promises but I will ask."

"Thank you, Detective."

"Goodbye, Riko-san."

"Goodbye." She walked Watanabe to the door and leant against the frame as he replaced his shoes and left, climbing into his car to drive away. First the car itself and then its light was lost in the glow of the streets. She locked the door and dragged her feet back to the kitchen. The blessing of sleep called but there was something she had to do first.

Riko picked up the phone and dialled. It wouldn't be too late back home and Mum always kept the phone near –

"Hello?"

"Mum, it's me." She paused. "Can I speak to Dad?"

Acknowledgements & Author's Note

Thanks first to my wife Brooke, who always sees the things I miss and who makes every story I write better, including *A Whisper of Leaves*.

Special thanks also to Eri Shinagawa, Na Gu and Elise Malberg for their endless patience with my questions about Japan and Japanese culture. Any faults in my research are my own in that regard, and I must credit them with the accuracies. Again to the Alchemists (CJ, Tess & Rebekah) whose input remains top notch and to the many readers and writers who also helped me: Nez, Gary, Allison, Jack, Chris and Erena, thank you each!

And gratitude also goes to the wonderful Amanda J Spedding for pushing me again to make the story stronger and David Schembri for most welcome assistance with formatting the ebook.

Finally to the brilliant Rebekah for coming up with another amazing cover!

Ashley

Note: For readers familiar with the 5-7-5 haiku tradition, I have used the EL approach which is broader, owing to the differences between Enlgish syllables and the Japanese *on* or 'morae' which are more dynamic than syllables. For instance, in English the word "haiku" has two syllables—"hai-ku", but in Japanese it's made up of three *on* and so it becomes "ha-i-ku". This usually results in EL haiku appearing 'shorter.'

About Ashley

Ashley is a poet, novelist and teacher living in Australia. Aside from reading and writing, he loves volleyball, Studio Ghibli and *Magnum PI*, easily one of the greatest television shows ever made.

You can find him online at @Ash_Capes or on his fiction blog, www.cityofmasks.com and at www.ashleycapes.com for poetry.

Also by Ashley Capes

Fiction

The Fairy Wren

The Bone Mask Trilogy
1. *City of Masks*
2. *The Lost Mask (forthcoming)*
3. *Greatmask (forthcoming)*

Poetry

pollen and the storm
stepping over seasons
orion tips the saucepan
between giants
old stone
7 Years

9 780099 2553722